When the Embrace Whispers

A heartwarming novel about unexpected turns, rediscovering passion, and tango

By Dimitris Bronowski

You are now the proud owner of this special launch edition of the book, having purchased it during the initial days of its release. To **discover the unique gifts exclusively reserved for owners of this version**, please visit whentheembracewhispers.com/resources today.

DEDICATION

To Tango,

You have brought happiness, friendships, love, family, trips, smiles, and unforgettable moments into my life. I hope that as more people discover what you have to offer, you'll do the same for them.

There are hugs that last
Way after they are done.
Hugs that embrace us,
And decide to stay, somehow, forever.
Hugs that stay,
That pick us up,
Not because we were down,
But because they saw more in us.
Gifts of a beautiful life,
Blankets in the cold,
That touch our surface,
But warm our inside.

Dimitris Bronowski
Author of Tangofulness and TheCuriousTanguero.com newsletter

The tango community is filled with wonderful people, always ready to embrace, help, and support. Many individuals have contributed, directly or indirectly, to making this book a reality. Thank you for believing in my vision to bring more people to tango.

A'lan Abruzzo, Abdullah Eracar, Acacio Coelho, Achim Schaller, Açucena Bix Khalifa, Adeline Masson, Aditya Mukherji, Adrian Bray, Adriana Agapie, Adriana Pegorer, Agata Bo, Agata Gąsiorowska, Agata Saga, Agis Petrides, Agne Lietuva, Agnieszka Sankowska, Agnieszka Szczepanowska, Ahmed Amr Farid, Aigars Strezs, Ajit Bubber, Ajla Doljančić, Al Villanueva, Alannah Ghazal, Alberto Barsellini, Alejandro Barriga Latinmania, Aleksandar Hristov, Aleksandra Perkowska, Aleksandra Spirkovska-Zlatanovska, Aleksey Vays, Alex Boon, Alex Kendall, Alex Podesta, Alexandra Cooke, Alexandru Eftimie, Alexia Nissiforou, Alice Pollak, Alice van Schagen, Alicia Noemi Carreiro Kon, Alison Myra Ozer, Alla Kotler, Alla Rabinovich, Amaia Amaya, Amanda Hamilton, Amanda Miranda-Flores, Amelia Marroquin, Amparo Ferrari, Amr Deyab, An Na, An Selm, Ana Franklin, Ana Szoc, Anand D'Souza, Anastasia Damoulianou, Anastasiya Bolkhovitinova, Andrea Béres, Andrea Doria Shaw, Andrea Martinez, Andrea Shepherd, Andreas Kemper, Andreas Schlaak, Andreea Achimescu, Andrejs Ljunggren, Andres Amarilla, Andrew Bock, Andrw Krl, Andrzej Bakula, Andy Heath, Anet Verdonk, Anette Berg, Anette Schamuhn, Angel Fernando González, Angel M, Angela Brandi, Angela Carol Ryan, Angela Cassan, Angela Errington, Angelina Pego, Angi Flacks Olguin, Ani Andreani de Herrera, Anjelika Brovkina, Ann Parker-Way, Anna Andreeva, Anna Burell, Anna Chourdaki, Anna Cristina L, Anna Fedorenko, Anna Kossak, Anna Löfgren, Anna Malenkov, Anna Norlin, Anna Poulaki, Anna Prostrollo, Anna Raiz, Anna Takkula, Anna Zadeh, Anne Baudrier, Anne Marie, Anni Sundqvist, Annie Bertolone, Annie Shaver-Crandell, Annika Estna, Anra Högemann, Antal Havasi, Antal Schweitzer, Anthea Okereke, Anthony Boccella, Antoaneta Mandajieva, Antónia Nagykáldi, António Cavaleiro, Antonio Eduardo Luz, Antonis Toulampis, Anželina Orgusaar, Ápsara Gartner Álvarez, Arianna Bottinelli, Arie Klok, Aris Psaltis, Arthur Waine, Asa Janson, Åsa Johansson, Asen Petrov Dimitrov, Asko Santala, Aslı Mertan, Aude Muller, Áurea Sánchez, Ave Ikadoil, Avi Win, Aykut Kazanci, Aziz Cinar, B Tango, Balinda Craig-Quijada, Barbara Brath, Barbara Merlotti, Barbara van Male, Barbara Wypart, Basil Barrett, Batt Johnson, Be Majed, Beata Broniek-Kęska, Beatriz Mackin, Bedish Tatlisu, Békés Anita, Belén Naw, Belen Rodríguez Pehovaz, Belisa Morillo, Benjamen Hansen, Berna Cantekin, Betsy Guerrero, Bianka Starzyńska, Bill Froud, Birgitta Schéle, Birgitte Drud, Birgitte Tirsvad, Birkit Biki Wildenburg, Björn Strander, Bo Norrman, Bob Dalziel, Bob Murray, Bojan Tosic, Bojana Zemunovic, Bonita Aalders, Branko Malovic, Brenda Barceló, Brick Robbins, Brigitte Lecadet, Buck Butler, Camilla Karlsson, Candy Bell, Cara Malli, Carla Anglehart, Carlos Di Sarli, Carlos Peralta, Carmela Schamps, Carmen Cordiviola, Caro Li Na, Carol Huxley, Carole Abdel-Massih Haddad, Caroline Reid - Artist, Carolyn Moss, Caron Malecki, Caryn Love, Catherine Antonelli, Céline Devèze, Celya Amparo Guajardo Tzotzolakis, Centro Artístico Analco, Cesar Bustamante, Chantal Dejardin, Chara Elmar, Charles Petitjean, Charles Scarrott, Che Tango, Che Wu Wei, Cheryl Blandin, Cheryl Macleod, Chhavi Mathur, Chiara Geishilla, chris barnett, Chris Bellekom, Christer Jansen, Christian Ceballos, Christian Marbach, Christian Martínez, Christian Paschen, Christiana Neofytou, Christina Branigan, Christina Kartsoli, Christina Sarioglou, Christine Sampson, Christos Kouroupetroglou, Christy Byers, Chuck Havranek, CiCi Shi, Claire Colliard, Claire Portalès, Clarisa Cruz, Claudia Danciu, Claudia Reuter, Claus Baer, Clay Marshall, Clf

Fontecilla, Coby Watier, Colette Flahaut, Colin Ratcliffe, Colleen Smith, Connie Collins, Conny Larson, Corina Covasa, Corinne Rover-Parkes, Crista Pisicista, Cristina Ferreira, Cristina Puscas, Cristy Gómez, Crystal Zhiying Dai, Csaba Purszki, Csilla Horváth, Dalie Green, Damián Dell'Amico, Dana N Pauline Drover, Danaë Etw, Danelle Knapp, Daniel Arokium, Daniel de Kay, Daniel Pereyra, Daniela Arcuri, Daniela Borgialli, Daniela Nossa, Daniela Stošić, Daniele Neri, Danielle Duhaime, Darko Mihailovic, Darko Radulovic, Darren Miles, David Grigonis, David Kovacs, David Phillips, David van Hemelryck, Dawn Kaye, Deanne Wilson, Deborah Rosén, Déborah Rupert, Debra Eliowitz Skiba, Debra Redcliffe, Dee Reilly, Deisy Orozco, Demetrio Scafaria, Denier D Or, Denis Roederer, Depy Perpinia, Derek Tang, Derrick Del Pilar, Desislava Obreshkova, Despina Sarri, Despoina Kr, Despoina Potouri, Di De Anna, Dia Dumitru, Diana Exante, Diana Feliz Mourão, Diana Pop, Diana Tique Ceballos, DiBe Bryson, Dima Arinkin, Dimis Toktok, Dimitra Plessa, Dimitris Bretas, Dimitris Moustaferis, Dirk Schmidt, Diva Carvalho, DJ BYC Bernardo, Do Ma Sza, Doina Ana, Domi Laure, Dominika Sefton, Dominique Bernard, Don Heilbrun, Don Peterson, Doris Von Der Aue, Dorothy Miranda Littell, Drew Martin, Drew Moir, Duddie David Mancini, Editha Ignacio, Eduard Gindin, Eduardo Drake, Eduardo Sidi, Eemia Enilec, Efi Parpa, Eiichi Chihara, Eileen Carson, Eirin Julia Marwitz, El Espejero, Elaine Gray, Eleanor Durrant, Elena Annis, Elena Drašković, Elena Koulikova, Elena Ryabova, Elena Sakhterova, Eleni Chimonidou, Eleni Kanira, Eleonora Duarte, Eliane Samba, Elias Georgiou, Elif Onural, Elina Eleni Gagari, Eline van Rijn, Elisa Hoekstra, Elisabeth Johansen, Elizabeth Mosher, Elli Andrea, Elli Dadira, Elodie Baran, Elodie Labonne, Elżbieta Kopeć, Elzbieta Manowiecka, Elzo Smid, Emeli Piccardo, Emiliano Farinella, Emine Akı, Emma Gonzalez, Eric A, Eric Arthur, Erico Crowther, Erin Donaldson, Espen Gees, Esra Karça, Eugene Theron, Eugenia Feka, Éva Hemrich, Eva Maria Agruña Barrón, Eva Marie TDj, Eva Provedel, Eva Srncová, Eve Williamson, Evi Chatziangelidou, Evren Jülide Koç, Ewa Andrearczyk, Ewa Bujak, Ewa Magier, Ewa Teresa, Ezio Piumatti, Fa Tima, Federico Poetto, Felicia McGarry, Felicity Tango, Fenia Pardalidou, Fernando De Lutiis, Fernando Robles, Filipp Knight, Fish AF, Floarea Mercea, Florencia Gil Bilbao, Foteini Georga, Fotini Karamanoli, Francesca Dih, Francesca Triani, Francisco Monteiro, Francisco Perez Luque, Franco Cesare Augusto Ottaviano, Francoise Ghillebaert, Françoise Jacquier, Frank Kirkpatrick, Frans Brom, Frantz Jozsef Sebestyen, Franz Alvaro Bravo, FX GA, Gabbo Fresedo, Gabe Brady, Gabriel Zambrano, Gabriela Trache, Gabrielle Steinberg, Gaelle Bidault, Gail Stoeger, Galatia Kontou, Galina Belova, Galina Shoub, Garyfalia Mavrou, Geertrui Luycx, Genevieve Picquart, Geoff Walker, George G Mirabal, George Mckee, Georgia Levaki, Georgina Disney, Gerd Braun, Gergana MamaLoca Boeva, Gherlando, Gi Sardinha, Giasafakis Michael, Gillian Adendorff, Gio Magneto, Giorgio Persos, Giorgos Hatzidakis, Giovanni Gherardini, Giovanni Maggio, Giulia Viniconis, Gloria Porta, Glynn Nicholas, Gneracion Tango, Goetz Hinrichsen, Gogo Chalkiadaki, Gold E Locks, Gordon Fong, Gorgios Linardos, Gosia Myc, Graham Guy, Graham Kite, Graham YS Kung, Grietje Pottie, Grigoris Karamperis, Gry Strømme, Grzegorz Łuczak, Gudrun Mellberg, Guillermo Brizuela, Gulja Iskhakova, Gunay Yetik Anacak, Gunbritt Mukti Mars, Gunilla Windon, Hana Ripp, Hanadi Jab, Hanan Sanaa, Hanna Backman, Hanna Ian, Hannes Koenig, Hans Freudenreich, Hans Peter Meyer, Harvey Schwartz, Haso JJ, Hayley Horn, Hazar Harba, Hazel Parry, Hector L Zeballos, Heike Renz, Heikes Sekieh, Helena Blumenthal, Helene van den Besselaar, Helga Sarah Will, Helio Woźniak, Henning Tango, Herbert Kampkuiper, Hernan Dionysus Ohaco, Hev Mate, Holger Hasten, Holger Svensson, Howard Frith, Ian Gay, Ian Turner, Ilektra Papachatzaki, Ilia Birba, Ilona Milonguera, Inci Yilmaz, Inga Kramarenko, Inge Bakker, Inge Locatango, Ingrid Van Deurzen, Ingrida Steponaviciene, Ioan Caulea, Ioana Dalca, Iordanis

Romaidis, Iqbal Mobarik, Ira Huber, Irene Jahnz Erickson, Irina Bazule, Irina Tanenbaum, Irina Tarkovskaya, Irini Kosta Sarika, Irit Sharon, Irmina Kaczor-Kwiatkowska, Iryna Kravchuk, Isabel Jimenez Acquarone, Isabelle Yu, Isalou Deslalpes , Ismena Ładecka, Israel Andalon, Iva Vukadinovic, Ivan Martin, Ivan Vickosis, Iwona Tempowski, Iwona Wojciechowska, J Alberto Patiño M, Jacek Kajakowiec, Jacek TuvoQue, Jack Hall, Jacqueline HM, Jacqueline Shorey, Jacques Chammas, Jade Draper, Jaime Juarez, James Ankiewicz, James Archambault, James Mason, James Valentino, Jamie Roberts, Jamila Zahran, Jan Even Evensen, Jan Krynický, Jan Van Belleghem, Jan Willem Troost, Jana Sigmundová, Janeen Yohann, Janet Earl, Janet Lott, Janetta Murrie, Jarno Tanskanen, Jasmin Kossenjans, Jasminka Bratulić, Javier Antar, Javier Marzello, Jay Ellerton, Jay Scheffers Okf, Jeanie Cutler, Jeanne Walker, Jef Mason, Jeffrey Simon, Jelena Kovačević Mezek, Jelezova Anna, Jenni Elo, Jennifer Hudson, Jennifer Koroskenyi, Jennifer Mabus, Jennifer Solheim, Jennifer Wrenn Kozar, Jenny Kirillova, Jesica Cutler, Jesper Sahlin, Jessyca Haas, Jeune Daleman Homme, Jim Baker, Jim Bulgatz, Jimena Zapata Micropigmentadora, Jimi ChimiChurri, Jiya Deora, Joan Green, Joanna Szymczewska, Joanne Zhou, Johan Gustafsson, Johan Kj, John Kraus, John Lloyd, John Newton, John Pashalidis, John Savidis, John Singletary, Jola Kaneary, Jon Peet, Jon Sørtvedt, Jonhy Aaron Pugh, Jorge Lladò, Jose Franco, Jose Stankovic, Josefina Zalasar, Joyce Cheng, Juan Cabral, Juan Carlos Vallejo, Juan Stefanides Tango, Jude Rose, Judit Ágnes Kiss, Judith Prister, Jukka Laajarinne, Julia Bless, Julia Courtney, Julia Hermansson, Julia Johnson, Julia Marley Bengtsson, Julia Ringrose, Julia Sky, Julian Ingram, Julian Metcalf, Julian Visch, Julie Cação, Julie Jenkins, Julie Winyard, Julien Peetermans, Julieta Benegas, June-Elleni Laine, Jurni Roco, Kaan Yildirim, Kakia Supresa Maragkaki, Kalina Duffner, Kalliopi Giagkopoulou, Kalman Bekesi, Kamil Wieprzowski , Kanwal Syed, Kareen Fellows, Karen Coleman, Karen Lewis, Karen Lyons, Karen Osen Isdal, Karen Russell, Karin Andersson Munthe, Karin Källström, Karolina Östlund, Karolina Wierzbowska, Kasia Katarzyna, Kate Fenton, Katherine Suazo Mellado, Kathy Lu, Kati Peltomäki, Kati Salo, Katia Iankova, Kay Anne Thomson Menzies, Kelly Richardson, Kenneth Schafermeyer, Kerry Bergen, Kevin Limbert, Kian Dwyer, Kiki Katzoli, Kim van Egmond, Kimberley Griffin, Kimberly Riggan, Kimberly Sue White, Kiran Anand, Kiran Sheena Premnath, Kirill Miniaev, Klara Eiswirt, Klaus Seidenfaden, Knud Stroem Nielsen, Kostas Poulos, Kovács Orsolya Tünde, Kręzi Kręželokk, Kristin Dion, Kristina Bak, Kristof Elst, Krisztina Nagy, Ksenia Mus, Ksenija Ristic, Kuba Gwizdała, Lacie Forde, Ladsi T Drover, Larry Clark, Las Hormigas Niños Artistas, Latife Y Matthis Tango, Laura Morrow-Dennis, Laura Wilkat, Laura Zeta, Laurel Leverton, Lawrence Beazley, Lazar Ilchev, Leah Bohle, LeAnn Lewis, Lechoslaw Hojnacki, Lee Nah Lim, Leen Peetermans, Leif Tjärnstig, Lele Luna, Lena Lindh, Lena Ogulnik, Lenny Hoeks, Leon Eakins, Leonhard Jaschke, Liana Maria, Lida Ravaglia, Lidija Stermecki, Liene Oberwahrenbrock, Liesbeth Bennett, Ligia Stanca Muntianu, Lilia Papadimitriou, Linda Bronzan, Linda Flynn Beekman, Linda Foster, Linda Hassan, Linda Wilton, Lis Hammeraa Nielsen, Lisa Fernow, Lizbeth Hamlin, Lloyd Spencer, Loisa Donnay, Lolli Santini, Lone Nielsen, Lorenzo Mantovano, Lorenzo Salzano, Los Locos, Louis Heath, Lucas Malec, Lucia Catană, Lucian Ionita, Lucian Stan, Luciano Des, Lucio Gobbo Tango, Lucja Abrams, Luis Enrique Uribe Gonzalez, Luis Rosado, Luisa Cardoso, LY Bao-Loan, Lyn Oates, Mada Vaitis, Magda Iwanicka, Magdalena Mari, Mahmoud Tango, Mai Elsheikh, Maja Đukanović, Malcolm Lafolley, Malgorzata Rokicki, Manal Kharrat, Manchoon Chan, Manna Geist, Manoj Unni, Manolis Founargiotakis, Manuel Fernandes, Mapu Llanten, Mar Azur, Mara Gucci, Mara Presecan, Marcelo Novo, Marco Reale, Marea Teuber, Margaret O'Riordan, Margaret Reeves, Margot Payne, Maria Ana Moira House, Maria Daskalaki, Maria Eliseeva, Maria

Fierro, Maria Iliopoulou, Maria Kamitsou, Maria Kazakidou, Maria Koletti-Mary Colettis, Maria Kovar, Maria Liliana Doval, Maria Maragaki, Maria Oikonomopoulou, Maria Pappas, Maria Paz Villarreal, Maria Pilar Falcao, Maria Simões, Maria Synti, Maria Tavantzopoulou, Maria Victoria Badin, Maria Winterman, Maria Zoumpouli, Mariana Orozco, Marianne Leszczynski, Marianne Schou, Mariano Laplume, Maribel Garcia Lindo, Marie de Milonga-Rhuys, Marie Ghantous, Marie McMillan, Marie Olofsson, Marie Patureau, Mariella Mattia, Mariet Ta, Marietta Garezou, Marilien Legrand, Marilu Arcaya Lopez, Marilynn Weiland, Marina Micanovic, Marina Misailidi, Marina Molina, Marina Parashchenko, Marina Vitanova, Marinda le Roux, Mario Silva Tango, Mariola Pantelic, Marion Bonnet, Marios Kyriakou, Marisa Costa, Marius Latinis, Marius Wrobel, Marjatta L Eladhari, Mark Carey Rees, Mark Chan, Mark McCormick, Mark Mindel, Mark Waters, Mark Word, Markus Fux, Marla Moffet, Marta Santos Lima, Marta Scho, Marta Zielinska, Martin Frohlick, Martin Grey, Martin Schwutke, Martin Topping, Martin Walters, Martin Wessels, Martyn Phillips, Mary Lourdes Silva, Mary Swingler, Massimiliano Civino, Mateusz Maksymiuk, Mathis Reichel, Matias Cosso, Matt Neverland, Matteo Manferdini, Matthew Qui Tango, Matthew Seneca, Matthias Kroll, Matthias Tango, Matthieu Stocks, Maturino Mariconte, Maurice Delaney, Maurice Watts, Mauricio Fuentes, Maurizio De Martis, Meg Thomson, Mei Klugman, Melinda Wetzel, Melisa Sacchi, Melissa Fitch, Meni Fotara, Menia Thomas, Mentore Siesto, Merica Mirošević, Metin Cobanoglu, Mi Lena, Michael Adam-Smith, Michael C, Michael Dorego Estacio, Michael Golde, Michael Hodgson, Michael Hulek, Michael Misiu Gniady, Michael N Mavros, Michael Parker, Michael Poole, Michael Rühl, Michael Thiele, Michał Hoppel, Michalis Chatzipanos, Michalis Georgopoulos, Michel Tomy, Michèle Drivon, Michele Tarquini, Michele Wucker, Michelle Browning, Michelle Harrison Morehouse, Michelle M-IxChel, Mieke Marianne, Mila Grosa Vigdorova, Mila Rakcevic, MilaGrosa Vigorosa, Milan Maksimovic, Milena Sparkles, Milo Radulovic, Milonga de La Confesión, Milonga LaRochelle, Mimí Crisante, Mina Elizabeth Montez Dumont, Mina Legnered, Minerva Pritchard, Mirco Capozza, Mire Vlad, Miriam Y Luis Rozenszajn, Mitali Sheekha Chinmulgund, Moïra Oeuvray, Mojca Mandem, Mone Loïse, Monika Jankowska-Kapica, Monika Ju Ka, Monika Parker, Monika Przyborowska, Moor Moor, Mounieb Ahmad, Muhamed Salem, Nadezhda Ilina, Nan Tanda'mi, Nar Cisee, Natalia Kunikowska, Natalia Nk Kalita, Natalia Soledad Petsalis, Natalie Debono, Natalie Pinchen, Natalka Kolody, Natasa TangoFlam, Natasha Eracleous, Natassa Karandinou, Nathan Hook, Neal McNamara, Nedda Viscovich, Negar Momtaz Jahromi, Nena Fernezir, Nermeen Baher, Nessie Komjathy, Nevin Tolba, Nick Jackson, Nick Shaforostov, Nick Shaw, Nicola Abbas, Nicola Perdriau, Nicoleta Deac, Nicoletta Pedicti, Nicușor Leca, Niki Papapetrou, Niko Carambas, Nim Naomi, Nina Santos, Noelia Barsi, Noelia Sorokin, Noemi Currier, Nora G Ponce, Norbert Rottmann, Noriko Muraoka, Olesea Andrei, Olesia Maksymiv, Olesya Krakhmalova, Olga Beid, Olga Dányi, Olga Novak, Olga Rodriguez, Olga Zherebetskaya, Olivier Comet, Olta Canka, Olya Less, Ondřej Vojtěchovský, Ophelia Giokarinis, Orestis Dimitriou, Orfeas Zafiris, Orlando Tango, Oscar Squire, Osváth Csilla, Otilia Bianchi, Otilia Turcanu, Outi Broux, Oxana Gouliaéva, Oxana Kovalenko, Ozan Bulut, Pablo Boccassino, Pablo Carnelutto, Pablo Cortazzo, Paco DobleGiro, Padmaka Mirihagalla, Pálffy-Balogh Márta, Pamela Beranek, Pamela J Tatarowicz, Pan Kowalski, Panos Georgopoulos, Para Dos, Pascale Pelsmaeckers, Patricia Evelin Avila, Patricia Gundert, Patricia Monica Vahanian, Patrick Maasen, Patrizia De Luca, Patty Velez, Paul Aitchison, Paul Ashburner, Paul Beard, Paul Holland, Paul Savoie, Paul Tupciauskas, Paula Barceló Aguilar, Paula Bosch-Johansson, Paula Duarte, Pauli Paulina, Pedro Andrés Sandín, Pedro Mendes, Pedro Rolo, Peggy R Johnson, Pekka Röksä, Peter Corvo Tdj, Peter Elias Knudsen, Peter Milligan,

Peter Okell-Walker, Peter Råndæl, Peter Rose, Peter Ruevski, Peter Simoneau, Petia Brainova, Petra Neumeyer, Petros Kampouridis, Philip Bodenstaff, Phill Rowbottom, Pia Sappl, Pierre-Olivier Bonnet, Piotr Bartha, Piotr El Buzo, Piotr Lamers, Pippa Cann, Plamen Ignatov, Politimi Kitsidi, Prabhath Sirisena, Predrag Stanojević, Prince Sohail, Quinn Saab, Radek Konarski-Mikołajewicz, Ramiro Villapadierna, Randy Cervantes, Raul Masciocchi, Ray Rudowski, Raymond Felix, Rement Theodora, Remy Vermunt, René Bøgh-Larsen, Ricarda Siebold, Ricardo Ferreira, Richard Beed, Richard Frisart, Richard Hatfield, Richard Houghton, Richard Lamberty, Richard Miller, Risa Benson, Rita Berenshteyn, Rob Bielak, Rob Jansen, Rob van der Woude, Robert Darwen, Robert Kostra, Robert Mazzucchi, Robert Schols, Robert Somme, Robert Z Tangowa, Roberta Forneris, Roberta Treves, Robin Tara, Rocky Madafferi, Roger Fickling, Roman Mohar, Rose C Donnelly, Rosemary Russo, Roula Tarina, Rumiana Yotova, Russell Shields, Rūta Slavinska, Ruth Hobbs, Ruxandra Jurca, S, Sabina Đogić, Sabina Fleschutz, Sage Agbonkhese, Salah Badie Gomaa, Sally Diakoloukas, Sam Plummer, Sam Woodward, Samantha Horan, Samantha Lambert, Samuel Mann, Sandra Ralha Dos Santos, Sandra Uri, Sara Francesca, Sara McElwain, Sara Sunshine, Sarah Angleryd Göller, Sarah Brown, Sarah McIntyre, Sarah Morgan, Sarah Vonthron-Laver, Sarianna Tammilehto, Sarkis Nalbandian, Sasa Grünbein, Saša Staparski Dobravec, Saša Živković, Sasha Kay, Sean Mcguigan, Seba Canto, Sebastian Paiza, Seda Gr, Serdar Kaplan, Serena Tango Lembach, Shahin Shokati, Sharon Waterson, Sharon Zamore, Shékhar Milonguero, Shelley Ward Cartier, Sherry Dickson, Shreya Shah, Shunyam van Steveninck, Sian Fussell, Sidewalktango, Sieg Mann, Silvia Askenazi Tango, Silvia Raulera, Silvio Cipriani, Simon Janrob, Simona Spada, Simone Schlafhorst, Simone Truhn, Sinóros-Szabó Botond, Sissi Terre, Siv Boström, Slava Yuta Maks, Slavomír Šahin, Slobodan Leo Bozic, Snejina Flowers, Sofia Mendes, Sofia-Sonia Christodoulou, Solmaz Bas, Solomon Burke, Sona Khachikyan, Sonja Unterwegs, Sonja Zivanovic, Sophia de Lautour, Sophia Georgiakaki, Sophie Heurtel, Søren Godik Godiksen, Søren la Cour, Sotiris Trantopoulos, Spiros P Riggas, Spyros Frantzeskakis, Stefan Löfgren, Stella Baker, Stella Dim, Stella M, Stella Yiannis, Stephanie Rae Meece, Stephen Crosbie, Steve H O G, Steve Littler, Steve Murphy, Steve Ricardo Aitken-Mellers, Steve Sewell, Stina Sundell, Stuart Schmukler, Subin Cleetus, Sue Birley, Sue Plummer-Mansell, Sue Walker, Susan Ryde, Susanna Krivulis, Susanne Bähring, Susanne Helalat Tango Querido, Suvi Vienonen, Sveta Lesnovskaya, Svetik Panarina, Svitlana Pochatenko, Sylvain Tango II, Sylvia Dorn, Sylvia Ontaneda-Bernales, Sylvie Sims, Sylwia Kijewska, Szkis Lex Poon, Szymon Ferfecki, Tamar Kasparian, Tamara de Graaff, Tamer Hafez, Tamy Markuz, Tangaurent Laurent Tran, Tango Bear, Tango Milonguer, Tango on the Rocks, Tango Pepe, Tango Seq, Tangralaa Jotan, Tanguero Harry, Tataru Cornel- Lusu, Tatiana Tikhonova, Tatjana Liliana Rossi, Tatyana Adeeva, Tatyana Nesterova, Teresa Bojarska, Teresa Elguezabal, Terho Antila, Terry Sca, Tetiana Khramova, Thanos Amar, Thanos Kasidis, Theodora Petrova, Theresa Gratton, Thijs van Veen, Thomas Mößner Tango Grafing, Tiberius Mitu, Tiffany Jackson, Tihamer Bogdan, Tijmen Wehlburg, Tim Hall, Tim Woolliscroft, Timi Pereira, Tina Leong, Tina Marie Tango, Tina Theodoritsi, Tino Tango, Tobias Bäumlin, Tom Hjelmgren, Tom Kamrath, Tom Opitz, Tomas Timoteusson Ekvall, Tomáš Wroblowský, Tomek Kopinski, Tomek Kulinski, Tommi Vornanen, Torbjörn Hornliden, Trevor Gillett, Tristan Adolphe, Tuna Mutis, Tzvetelina Miltchova Stefanova, Udo Fekken, Ugo De Falco, Uli Tango, Ulla Ritamäki, Unni Hermansen, Ursula Fischer, Valeria Cressati, Valerie Williams, Valia Kostakou, Vanja Maslovarik, Vasanthi Vanniasingham, Vasilis Psomos, Vely Daleus, Venla Kurra, Venla Sipilä-Rosen, Vera Futorjanski, Verena O'Neill, Verica Sambolec, Veronique Vassard, Veselinka Georgievska, Vicki Chaudoin Kamerer, Vicky Damianou, Victor Banzon, Victor

Munteanu, Victoria Hartviksen, Victoria Henriquez, Victoria Luna, Vildan Şener, Vince Frost, Vincenzo Alaimo, Violetta Ambrozuk, Virgil Herciu, Virginia Kelleher, Waldemar Strazdins, Walentyna Długaszewska, Walle Tere, Walter Barnes, Walter Huijten, Warren Edwardes, Wayne Evans, Wayne Rozier, Wendy Clowson Feinstein, Willem Wilson, William Hindenburg, Willie Linden van Der, Wim Warman, Wyn Maree, Xiaoi Tan, Yelena Shubina, Ylva Gustavsson, Youlie Mouzafiarova, Yves Mayrand, Zoya Parkansky, Zsolt Szenasi, Zsuzsanna Farkas, Zulfiya Jva, βασιλικη θεόδωρος χριστοδουλου, Γιάννα Κραββαρίτη, Γιωργία Κατρίνη, Γιώργος Κομνηνού, Δρ Κατερίνα Βολονάκη, Ειρήνη Κατσαμά, Εριέτα Χαρκουτσάκη, Ιρένε Λασηθιωτάκη, Κατερίνα Χατζιδάκη, Κιμουρτζή Αικατερινη-Στυλιανη, Μαρία Μαστρογιάννη, ΜΑΡΙΑ ΠΑΠ, Μιχάλης Νικηφοράκης, Παναγιωτάκη Πόπη, Παναγιώτης Πουλημενέας, Στέλλα Μπουμπουλάκη, Κρασимир Стоянов, Метју Спенсер, Миомир Боянич, Морога Виорика, Неда Вукадиновић, Оксана Дрозд, Светлана Овечкина, Симона Петкова, Цветослав Вучев, Юлиана Амелина, تانغوا دمشق.

Finally, a special thank you to a few of the subscribers of thecurioustanguero.com newsletter who were there for me when I asked for help:

Adrian, Alan, Alberto, Aleksandar Hristov, Alex, Alexandra Cooke, Alison Summers, Amanda, Ana, Ann, Ann Sophie, Anna, Anne, Artur Skupien, Astrid Vik Stronen, Aurea, Aurore, Aydan, Barbara, Barbara Trask, Batt Johnson, Beat, Beverley Hubbard, Bill, Bill Swan, Boglarka Ban, Boguslaw, Bonnie, Brett, Carl, Carmen, Caroline Falk, caron malecki, Charley, Chiara, Chris, Chris Tyler, Ciro, Cluadio, Colette Flahaut, Colleen Smith, Crista, Cristina Puscas, Daisy, Daniel Singer, Danka, Dario, Darwin, David, Debbie, Denis, Dennis, Doug, Drew, Ebony, Elaine, Élodie Labonne, En Kay, Evelyne, Evi, Foteini, Frank, Gabrielle, Guy, Hana Ripp, Hanna, Heidi, Isa, James, Javier Antar, Jean Pierre, Jean-marie, Jo, Joan, John, José, Jose Amador, JRae, Jürgen Schnitzler, Karin, Krisztina, Kylie Chan, Laszlo, Laurent, Laxmi, Leena, Lise, Lourdes, Luís Daniel Pinheiro da Silva, Lynne, Malvika, Marc, Mark, Markus, Marla, Michael, Michèle Drivon, Myszko Miauczy Pierwszy, Nicoleta Moroeanu, Nim, Nina, Olga, Päivi Toikkanen, Patricia, Peter, Rita Mhanna, Rodrigo, Saeed, Sandra Brintnall Katz, Sasha, Sasha, Silvio Cipriani, Susanne, Suzi, Svetlana Larri, Sylvie Brien, Thanos, Tony, Vanina, Veikko, Venceslava Marie Jarotkova, Victoria Fernandes, Wiebke, Yann, Yanni, Zsuzsa.

Chapter 1

Sarah's mobile vibrated on the coffee table, interrupting her distant gaze out the rain-streaked window. Mark's photo was on the screen with a big green button ready to be clicked. Sarah sipped her latte and looked up again. Raindrops drummed on the windowpane, echoing her restless thoughts.

As a teenager, she used to step out of the house and walk in the rain. Her mother never fussed about rain-soaked clothes or muddy shoes. "That's what stuff is for, to be used," she'd say with a smile. When Sarah returned home, her mother would welcome her and request she leave her shoes at the entrance. "There is no place for wet shoes inside the house. Now off to take a warm shower, princess."

However, today her thoughts were anchored in a more recent past. It all began five years ago, with fireworks of emotion and happiness a bit after her thirty-third birthday. In the initial months, she and Mark traveled on low-budget trains and buses, had picnics in the park, and took long walks by the beach. They moved in together quickly to save money. Discussions revolved around life, dreams, and having children. They even talked about Sarah leaving her unfulfilling job for a passion yet undiscovered. Yet, she had just received a promotion at the same job she had planned to leave—more money, less freedom, and more people to please.

As months turned into years, the initial excitement began to fade. She couldn't recall the last time they did something unexpected or new together. Financial struggles were no longer pressing, thanks to Mark, and they now had a splendid new house he had designed from scratch. A smile flickered on Sarah's lips as she recalled how Mark had unveiled their new home. Taking her to their new neighborhood, he asked her to close her eyes. Guiding her carefully, they ascended stairs, and upon entering the house, he led her to a room. Placing her hands on a table, she heard the sound of something metallic being set before her. Tracing it with her fingers, she felt the smooth,

1

matte finish and some sharp cuts along its edge. Opening her eyes, she stared at the key. "Welcome to our future," Mark said, his voice tinged with excitement. Sarah looked around, and her mouth dropped.

At the heart of the kitchen, a sleek black marble island doubled as a chic breakfast bar. State-of-the-art appliances adorned the kitchen, and glossy white furnishings surrounded her. In the beginning, they found themselves spending hours cooking and sharing meals there.

Sarah rushed outside. It was a two-story, red-brick townhouse nestled on a tree-lined street. "Seventh tree on the right," Mark said behind her. "You can plant flowers on the left side of the garden, outside the grass line," Mark said. "It's not a lot of space, but if we put more flowers, the grass won't align nicely with the wall lines."

"And what is that?" Sarah asked, pointing to a small baby swing in the corner. "That's... for later," Mark replied with a smile. Sarah's eyes welled up, and she hugged him tightly. "Hey, hey, one step at a time," Mark said.

They returned to the house. The living room was cozy, featuring a large bay window that allowed ample natural light to filter in. Upstairs, the tranquil bedroom featured a king-sized bed with soft, neutral linens, soothing blue walls, and a large window overlooking greenery. Next to it, a pastel-toned room housed a baby's rocking bed, still wrapped in plastic.

Not much had changed since then. Sarah attempted to place flowers in different spots, but Mark always moved them back to the designated area. The rooms remained the same, and the house was kept pristine by Samantha, their cleaning lady. The baby's room and swing remained unused. This thought left a pang of unfulfilled longing in Sarah's heart. One thing was different, though. Mark detested wasting time, and since they could afford it, the kitchen now primarily served as the spot for receiving food deliveries. It was a house of serene comfort, the kind that many of her friends would love to have.

Sarah took another sip of her coffee, ignoring the vibrating mobile. Her eyes drifted to the cafe's walls, adorned with the owner's life adventures. On the wall, she saw pictures of a hot air balloon ride above mountains, dancing in a dimly lit room with a woman in a red dress, finishing a marathon in an ancient stadium, visiting a market filled with colorful spices, and watching a flamenco show. She gazed at the pictures, as she had many times before, immersing herself in the imagined sensations of such a life—the crispness of cold mountain air, the symphony of bustling market noises, the thrill of exploring unknown streets. Yet, it was the photo of the red dress that resonated with her the most. The fluid movement of the dancer, her dress a cascade of crimson, had etched itself into Sarah's heart, evoking feelings she couldn't quite name but always longed to experience.

Turning her attention back to Mark's photo on the vibrating screen, she observed his tall and lean figure. His dark, neatly styled hair, occasionally slightly disheveled, added to his casual charm. It was his brown eyes with long eyelashes that Sarah fell in love with. Most women would kill to have eyelashes like those. Shifting in her seat, Sarah took a deep breath, closed her eyes, and clicked on the insistent green button.

"Is it a good time?" Mark asked.

"It's always a good time to talk with you," Sarah replied.

"How was work?"

"I had another fight with my boss. She doesn't want to accept any of my proposals. I don't understand what's the point of giving me the job and then not letting me decide anything."

"That's terrible. I'm sorry to hear that. You can tell me more at home. Listen, about the trip. I can't leave now. I have too many things to finish. We'll need to do it another time."

Another time. Sarah's free hand shifted, as if she were about to strike the table in front of her. She opened her eyes, realizing she had made contact with something. Coffee had spilled onto the floor and her shoes.

"Can I make it up with dinner tomorrow night?" Mark continued, "My favorite restaurant has an invited chef, 3 Michelin stars. You will love it."

"Who would say no to 3 Michelin stars?" Sarah said, her voice flat, as she futilely dabbed at the coffee spill.

"You'll love it. On your way back, please buy a Château Pontet-Canet, year 2016 if it's available. See you soon."

Sarah locked the mobile and placed it face down on a dry spot on the table. "Who would say no to 3 Michelin stars?" she repeated in a low voice, trying to remove the coffee stain from her shoes. Mark worked hard to provide a comfortable, calm life, she knew that. A life she couldn't have imagined creating on her salary. With him, she was safe. No man is perfect, but she felt he was as close to it as a woman approaching her forties could hope for. Traveling, children, and dreams could wait one more year. *Good enough*, she thought, looking at the half-cleaned stain on her shoes, *the rest will wash away with the rain.*

Chapter 2

Sarah popped open her umbrella, stepping out from the warm glow of the café into the evening chill. Walking in the city always made her feel insignificant. Nobody seemed to notice her. People walked briskly, absorbed in their own thoughts, while the urban environment bustled around them. Towering skyscrapers, historic edifices, and sleek glass structures defined the city's skyline, the kind of buildings that made her feel even smaller.

Usually, the city buzzed with a symphony of sounds. Horns honked as taxis weaved through traffic; the chatter of people and the calls of street vendors were an everyday part of it. But that night, the city felt a lot louder. Everybody was in a hurry to avoid the heavier rain predicted by the weather channel.

She looked at the street in front of her, the same street she had walked for years to get from her favorite coffee place back home. She could close her eyes and visualize every turn, every traffic light, every store. She used to take a different path until Mark decided to race her back home, telling her there was a faster way to get there. They laughed, made a bet, and started running. He was correct. Sarah hugged him at the end of the race, whispered "You are always right, aren't you?" in his ear, and then they went straight to the bedroom for an afternoon she would always remember with a smile.

Not today, she thought. She was not in a hurry to get back home, to see Mark, or to talk about her terrible day at work. She turned to the first corner she found. The street was empty. *Great*. She banged her hand on a wall and quickened her pace. She wanted to scream, but that would draw other people's attention. Left, right, left, right, left. The rain transformed from a drizzle to a torrential downpour, each drop splattering against the pavement, and the few people outside ran to get cover. As she turned around another corner, a taxi hit a road bump next to her, splashing her with dirty rainwater. Drenched, she looked down, her soaked clothes clinging to her. She locked eyes with the taxi driver, her gaze heavy with unspoken reproach, but he drove away, oblivious. "Nobody cares anymore," she muttered, and closed her umbrella, surrendering to the rain.

With each step, tears silently streamed down her face. She lifted her hand to remove them but stopped midway. Nobody would notice them either way. "Why? Why can't you just be happy? What's wrong with you?" she whispered. Something caught her eye. She looked to her right, noticing the mirror of a small local gym. And there she was. Streaked mascara trails ran from her eyes, painting a poignant picture on her cheeks, the rain and tears indistinguishable. Her shoes were now sullied and soaked through. She stood motionless, looking at her reflection.

The sound of the rain intensified. Water from a nearby building's guttering fell on a garbage bin, creating a chaotic symphony of beats. Sarah closed her eyes and wrapped her arms around herself. Her chest rose and fell. And then, she heard it.

A solitary piano note sliced through the air, soon joined by the sorrowful cry of a violin. *What crazy musician is still on the street?* The music seemed to pause briefly. Sarah took a few steps in the direction from which the sounds emanated. Another note. With every step, the music became clearer and louder, and oddly, older. The piano ceased, but the violin continued, slow and melodic. Sarah's eyes filled with tears once more. A void formed inside her chest, a longing. The music grew stronger, reached a crescendo, and then stopped.

A lone red light flickered at a building's entrance, like a beacon in her stormy night. *Red light?* She thought. *That can't be right.* She approached and reached the door. It was slightly open. Carefully, she pushed it a tiny bit and looked inside with one eye only. The music was definitely coming from there. She could hear people talking. A few seconds later, someone applauded. She positioned her ear at the slight opening of the door to listen better. And then she felt a hand on her shoulder. Sarah jumped.

"Excuse me, young lady, can I pass? Oh, wait. You are all wet. What are you doing out here? Come, with me, with me now."

A petite, elderly lady, her age etched gracefully in the lines of her face, seized Sarah's elbow with surprising strength, ushering her into the warmth.

"But..." Sarah started.

"I'll never understand your generation. Please, leave the shoes at the door. There is no place for wet shoes on the dance floor. Come on, come on, we have warm tea inside, and you are late."

Late? For what? With hesitant curiosity, Sarah edged closer, peering through the next door where a different world seemed to unfold. *OK, that's definitely a dance floor.* She took her shoes off.

"Come, let's get you out of these clothes." The old lady took her to the changing room. "Here, try this skirt. I don't have a good top for this. Well, young lady, you'll stay with your t-shirt, if you don't mind looking a bit sloppy."

"I don't even remember the last time someone called me a young lady," Sarah responded with a smile.

"Well, you haven't given me your name yet, have you, young lady? In my days, we used to give our names straight away."

"I am sorry. It's Sarah. And you are?"

"My friends call me Maria. This way, Sarah."

Maria took Sarah to the main dance hall. Dim, ambient lighting bathed the studio, a stark contrast to the bright, lively hues of her childhood dance memories. Chairs and a few tables surrounded the dance floor. Four guys were laughing in a corner, all wearing baggy pants. *A hip hop class? Can't be. Those pants are too elegant.* A few women were chatting on one side of the floor, and a few more were seated on the other side putting on their dance shoes. The shoes were also different from what Sarah remembered. Instead of the traditional pink color of the heels used in Latin dances, dance shoes of every hue dotted the room. Turquoise ones sparkling like the ocean, another pair adorned with delicate butterflies, and a glossy black pair gleaming under the soft light.

"You don't have high heels, do you?" asked Maria. "No worries, you can dance without them."

"Dance? I can't... I've never really learned."

"Isn't that what a dance class is for?"

A door on the other side of the studio opened. Sarah's mouth dropped open. A woman in her late twenties entered. She wore a long black dress with a huge opening on the side. Thin waist, long black hair, a massive smile, and long legs gracefully walking on top of a pair of red high heels. *Those look at least 9 cm.*

One of the guys from the group that Sarah hadn't noticed before clicked a few buttons on a computer on the side. The sounds of a violin filled the room. He approached the woman with the red shoes. He had a muscular build but moved with grace and agility. He was a bit taller than Mark, with a thick mane of jet-black hair that fell in loose waves. Sarah noticed the square jawline, the high cheekbones. His dark eyes were framed by thick eyebrows.

A second later, everything seemed to slow down. They took a deep breath and embraced each other. They stood there, hugging, for a few seconds. The woman was still smiling, but her eyes were closed. Then they moved together. The man took a few steps forward while she stepped backward, maintaining the embrace. They stopped for a moment, then started walking again. They completed a full circle around the dance floor before pausing again. They didn't stop hugging. Then the music became faster and more intense. In unison, they glided to the side, their movements a fluid echo of each other. The woman whirled around the man with grace, while he elegantly entwined one leg around the other. As she circled him, he unwound, his leg tracing a perfect arc on the floor. Her legs were here one moment, and in the next, his took their place. They spun in harmony, alternating directions, her legs occasionally slicing through the air. All the while, her smile never waned, her eyes remaining serenely closed. As the music mellowed, their movements followed suit, decelerating until the final note, where her leg entangled with his. In that moment, their embrace tightened, their faces inches apart. The music ceased, leaving only the rhythmic rise and fall of their chests, still deeply in sync with the lingering echoes of the song. He smiled. She opened her eyes. Everyone applauded as they slowly took a few steps away from each other.

Sarah watched, spellbound, her breath caught in her chest. Her eyes were fixed on this woman. Elegant, happy, beautiful, young. *Free*. And those red shoes...

The woman approached Sarah. "You might want to close your mouth," said Maria. Sarah swallowed.

"Bienvenida. Primera clase?" asked the woman.

Sarah froze. "Ahhhh, what, sorry, I don't speak..."

"Good evening," she interrupted. "Is this your first class?"

"Yes. Yes, first class," Sarah finally came back to herself. "Wow, that choreography, that was... That was amazing."

"No choreography there. Pure improvisation."

Sarah took a moment to absorb this. "So, you improvised every step?"

"That's the man's job. They've got to do their part so that I can do mine. You'll see. Everyone, find a partner now!"

Sarah froze for a second. *Find what now?* She had no intention of making a fool of herself in front of all those people after what she had just watched.

"Not you, honey. This is an advanced class. Come back on Wednesday. You can keep the skirt till then, but maybe get rid of that shirt," said the woman and walked away.

Sarah looked at herself in the mirror.

"Don't bother with her," Maria said almost apologetically. "Youth takes time to learn humility."

Sarah gave a sigh of relief and turned to leave the dance floor. She took one step and bumped straight into the man who was dancing a few seconds ago.

"Let's try one song, shall we?" he said.

She looked straight into his eyes. From that close, she noticed a shade of hazel, with a hint of green. They were sparkling in a way Sarah had never seen before.

He slowly put his right hand on her back. Instinctively, Sarah put her left hand around his neck. He took her right hand in his left and lifted it to the height of their shoulders.

"I don't know what to do," she whispered.

"Then don't do anything. We are not in a hurry."

9

Sarah closed her eyes. As she hugged him a bit tighter, she felt it again. A void inside her chest she couldn't explain.

She felt his body gently moving a tiny bit to the side and then back again. Without realizing how, she started switching her weight from one foot to the other. She followed, waiting for those first elegant steps that she saw before to happen. His embrace felt secure and yet comfortable, calm. She could move freely inside the embrace if she wanted. She could feel his body. It wasn't every day that she hugged a guy like this. Her heart started beating faster. She felt her face getting red. *Breathe. Get ready to walk.* Then she felt something else. She was uncertain at first. She took another deep breath. She could feel his heartbeat. It was slow but strong. One minute passed, then a second. Three minutes later, the song ended. Rooted in place, they moved not an inch, yet in that stillness, Sarah felt the void disappear.

"I am Diego," he said softly. "See you tomorrow at six."

"Yes, the... Tomorrow. This tomorrow. Yes, I'll be there. Here. I'll be here."

Maria took her hand and led her to the entrance to find her shoes. Sarah looked at her, only to see her huge smile.

"You felt it, didn't you?"

"What?"

"Tango."

Sarah nodded.

"It was waiting for you, for too long. Tango waits until we are ready. You are here now. Your time has come."

Chapter 3

The aroma of fried bacon wafted through the door, greeting Sarah even before her key clicked in the lock. Her face lit up with a smile, and she dashed indoors. Arrayed on the kitchen table was a culinary masterpiece: a generous bowl of pasta, its aroma hinting at a rich blend of veal and pork, alongside a plate artfully arranged with a tempting selection of soft and hard cheeses. Mark, still in his work attire, absentmindedly fiddled with a delivery bag before his gaze found Sarah.

"What happened to you? Are you boycotting umbrellas?" he chuckled, eyeing her damp hair.

Shoes flung off in a playful scatter, Sarah's footsteps echoed with haste towards the kitchen.

"You won't believe what happened. The rain, I was walking, there was a red light, the door was open..."

"Breathe," Mark interjected, placing his hands on her shoulders. "You're all wet. I don't want you catching a cold. Why don't you take a warm shower first? In 5 minutes, the food will be on the table, and you can tell me everything. Sounds good?"

"I'll be back in 3," Sarah said and raced to the bathroom. Her wet footprints shimmered under the white ceiling lights. She threw her wet clothes on the floor. As the water enveloped her, she closed her eyes and bowed her head, releasing a deep. Gradually, she shifted her weight from one leg to the other, humming the violin melody from the song Diego danced with his partner. She imagined herself gliding across the dance floor, pausing briefly to synchronize breaths with him, and then accelerating once more. In her mind's eye, she saw her legs moving gracefully—sometimes on the floor, sometimes in the air, occasionally brushing against his leg.

"Everything alright in there? The food will get cold, you know," Mark's voice, accompanied by a half-opened door, interrupted her reverie. Startled, Sarah jumped, feeling her face flush.

"Sorry, the warm water felt so good. Coming down in 2 minutes. I have so much to tell you," she said. As Mark's footsteps faded, a silent laugh escaped Sarah. She lingered in the shower's warmth, the echo of tango music playing in her mind. *Grow up, princess*, she chided herself. She slipped into the cozy embrace of her full-body pajamas, a thoughtful, warming gift from Mark. Her body temperature always ran a bit lower than most, so donning those pajamas, adorned with an array of cats, became one of her favorite rituals. Skipping down the stairs, she found the food arranged on the table, and Mark calmly reading a business magazine.

"It smells incredible. It's like I'm at a five-star hotel's restaurant, " she beamed.

"Thank you. I'm very skilled at typing our address on the app," Mark chuckled. "Did they have the wine?"

Sarah's eyebrows shot up, and she bit her lip in a playful pout, trying to look as guiltily adorable as possible.

"You know I can't be mad at you when you make those faces," Mark said, laughing. "No worries, I think I still have Chianti available," he said and left the room.

"Can I tell you, can I tell you, can I tell you?" Sarah said with excitement when Mark returned.

He nodded.

"I left after our call. I decided to take a different street than usual."
"Why?"

"No real reason, I just took a different path. And then it started raining. I... " She hesitated. "I had to find some cover from the rain. I entered a building, and there was music. It was a tango class," she said with a huge smile on her face.

"Tango? Like Antonio Banderas?"

"Yes. Well, no. It was different. They were dancing, but not jumping in the air or anything like that. They hugged, and then they moved together."

"Married couples?"

"Some of them, I guess, but not all," Sarah looked confused.

"I don't understand how any man would be okay with random guys hugging his partner. Poor guys. So, what happened?"

Sarah lifted her wine glass and brought it slowly to her mouth, staring at its ruby-red color. It felt drier than usual.

"The teachers danced. It was amazing. But... I guess you needed to be there to see it. I can't really describe it. Anyway, the rain stopped, and I walked back home. Sorry for forgetting the wine. But this one goes great with the meat. You do know how to pick them. Always right."

Mark smiled, lifted the bottle, poured a bit more into her glass, and began explaining what made Chianti such a good fit. Sarah moved her chair a few inches back and removed some imaginary lint from her pajama. Her gaze drifted and eventually settled on the deep red hue of the wine in her glass, a vibrant, mesmerizing color that seemed to dance and swirl with a life of its own. The rich scarlet of the wine evoked something distant yet intensely familiar. It harkened back to the woman in the red dress she saw in the photograph at the coffee shop. As Mark continued to expound on the virtues of the Chianti, Sarah's thoughts drifted further, carried away by the tide of her reverie, as she continued eating. The conversation became a distant hum, like background music to her inner world. The wine, the color, the sudden resurgence of a long-lost dream, it all coalesced into a singular urge. Once she finished her food, she excused herself, carrying the image of the red dress and the unseen dancer with her.

"I am going to sleep," she said and stood up. "I have to work early tomorrow."

The sheets crumpled beneath her as she allowed her body to collapse onto the bed. Rolling, she brushed a strand of hair away from her face and stared at the ceiling.

Her mobile on the nightstand vibrated once. As her fingers lightly brushed over the cool screen, she hesitated for a moment before tapping on the unlock button. The soft glow of her phone revealed a previsualization of the incoming message as her eyes skimmed the words. "I am going out for a run. If you need anything..." She didn't read the full message. She looked at the ceiling once more. And then, she turned her head slowly toward the phone one more time, and a smile appeared on her face.

She typed 'Tango' and a second later, an endless list of YouTube videos popped up. Videos from the movies Take the Lead and Scent of a Woman appeared, but she scrolled down. Her finger stopped when she saw a man who looked a bit like Diego. The thumbnail showed the man in a black suit, embracing his partner in a white dress. Hundreds of people had formed a big circle around them, watching. Her heart raced as her finger hovered over the play button. She never had the courage to dance in front of people she knew, let alone so many strangers. She clicked and waited impatiently for an ad to finish.

The couple was away from each other, on the opposite sides of a large dance floor. There were hundreds of people around them, standing or seated, quiet. The man lifted his hand, signaling something. A gentle crackle and pop filled the room. Sarah recognized this sound. Her father loved listening to vinyl discs when she was young. She remembered his face changing the moment he heard them. He knew that what came after this charming imperfection was real music, a portal to the warm and vintage ambiance of vinyl playback. 'Tiny, rhythmic footprints,' he used to call them. Then, the first notes struck. Sarah felt goosebumps forming on her. She couldn't tell what the instrument was. It sounded like an accordion, but its sound was distinctively different. The sound was rich, complex. She could feel the notes in her chest.

The dancers stayed still for a few seconds. Then the music became more rhythmic, and the man walked toward the woman with confidence. He stopped an inch away from touching her. The woman slowly placed her left arm around his shoulders and touched the back of his neck with her hand. She touched his chest with hers. His right arm went gently all around her back. Then he extended his left hand to the side. They both turned their heads toward the hand and looked at it. The woman lifted her hand and tenderly placed it on his. She closed her eyes and they took a deep breath together.

Sarah barely noticed their legs' movements as they danced. Her gaze remained fixed on the embrace and their faces. His expression seemed pained. *He loves her*, Sarah thought instinctively. The music slowed down, romantic and powerful simultaneously, as a singer started to sing. The woman's eyes remained closed, serene, as if she wasn't aware of the numerous pairs of eyes focused on her. She

14

adjusted her hand on her partner's neck, offering a gentle caress. Their lips momentarily hovered so close that Sarah thought they were going to kiss. In the final notes of the song, the woman broke away from the embrace, leaving him alone in the middle of the dance floor.

The video concluded, and Sarah remained motionless, fixated on the screen, breathing slowly. After a few seconds, she noticed the song's title, 'Fueron tres años.' It took her a moment to find the translated lyrics. The song portrayed a man realizing that three years had passed since his love left him. He implored her to break the silence, to grant him a moment to kiss her lips before he departed. Memories of their last kiss lingered. He called her 'my treasure.'

Sarah re-watched the video, feeling as if she were witnessing a different performance. She understood why he approached her, why their lips nearly touched, and why he stood alone in the center as the singer uttered the final word of the song: "adios." "Goodbye."

Sarah lost herself in the labyrinth of videos, each dance a whisper of something more, until her eyes surrendered to weariness. Opening the Clock app to confirm her morning alarm, she stared at the screen. Hovering her finger over the plus button, she took a deep breath and clicked. New alarm: 5:30 *PM*.

Chapter 4

"What do you mean you don't have it? I requested a guide for the tibial tunnel specifically for this surgery. We can't start without it."

Sarah looked into the doctor's bewildered eyes, realizing this was going to be one of *those* days.

"I'm sorry, it wasn't on the list I received," she mumbled, rifling through her bag for the document. "I'll text Laura to send it right away," she said and hurried out of the surgery room. It wasn't the first time such a situation had occurred. Doctors usually sent their surgical tool requests to Sarah's office a day in advance. Subsequently, someone would assemble the toolbag and deliver it to Sarah for transportation to the surgery room. Yet, mistakes like these were not uncommon. Despite it not being Sarah's responsibility to prepare the toolbag, and the doctors being aware of it, she found herself facing the doctors' irate expressions too often.

Closing the waiting room door, Sarah glanced at the patient lying on the bed, clad in a hospital gown. She knew he would have to endure at least an hour on that bed until the guide was delivered. Unaware that someone's inability to copy and paste a tool's name or read a list without skipping items was the cause of his prolonged wait, he would gaze at the fluorescent lights on the ceiling.

"Let me adjust this a bit," Sarah said with a smile, pulling a few levers. The top of the bed elevated, offering him more comfort and a better view of his surroundings.

'Tell the doctor to expect delivery by 5:15, 5:30 at the latest. I'll keep you updated,' Laura's message popped up on Sarah's screen. She relayed the message from her company's coordinator to the doctor and found a seat in the waiting room. Her Instagram feed showcased young, vibrant individuals in exotic swimming pools in countries she could only dream of. Others trekked on mountains with breathtaking views, sharing motivational quotes that reassured her of the endless possibilities. Sarah's thumb tiredly scrolled through her feed, the glamour of the virtual world dimming as boredom crept in. With a sigh, she placed her mobile in the pocket of her baggy green scrubs. *Couldn't they design something a tad bit sexier for us to wear?*

Across the room, Sarah's eyes fell upon the patient, his gaze locked on the white clock's red digits ticking away. A fleeting, unsettling thought crossed Sarah's mind, lingering longer than she expected. *What if she were in that bed, her own mobility a distant memory? What if she couldn't move?*

Her mobile vibrated. *Finally.* She stood up and left the room. Pulling the mobile from her pocket, she stopped. It wasn't a text from her coordinator. It was her alarm. 5:30. *Tango.* And she was still in the hospital, waiting, aware that she wouldn't be paid a dime more for this time spent. She pivoted and headed straight to the bathroom. In the mirror's reflection, Sarah saw the frustration etched on her face, her breath fogging up the glass momentarily as she exhaled heavily. Another vibration. 5:31. She took a deep breath and hurried down the stairs. Returning to the surgery room, she organized the tools next to the surgery table, attempting to catch her breath. She glanced at the clock's red numbers. 5:39.

The doctor arrived and inspected the tools. He put on jazz music and instructed the anesthesiologist to prepare the patient. Sarah had heard doctors play various genres during surgery, and jazz typically indicated a calm and relaxed atmosphere. She looked at him and he seemed to be in a much better mood. She realized this was her opportunity.

"Is it alright if I leave the tools here and head out?" Sarah asked, her voice tinged with hopeful urgency. The doctor looked at her. "I have an appointment, and it would be hard to reschedule," she explained, trying to look worried. The doctor signaled with his hands that she could leave. Sarah didn't wait a second longer. Once again, she ran.

As she turned on her engine, she felt grateful it wasn't raining. Traffic was such a mess when it rained. She was a careful driver, but today she was in no mood to play nice. A couple of orange traffic lights later, she found a parking spot five minutes away from the dance studio. The car's clock showed 6:01 before it switched off.

17

Sarah arrived breathless at the entrance of the studio. A mix of laughter and music filled her ears. Diego was in front of the mirror chatting with a couple of women, while the rest of the people were putting on their shoes. He turned his head toward her.

"Sarah!" he exclaimed happily and walked quickly toward her across the dance floor with a huge smile on his face. "You are not wet anymore."

"Yes, although I am sweating a bit," Sarah laughed. "I thought I was late."

"Tango waits," Diego winked at her. And then, pretending he was some kind of sophisticated preacher, he continued, "Never run behind a man, a train, and a tango class. There will always be more."

"I have to write this down," Sarah said, pretending she was looking for a notepad.

Diego looked at her and laughed. "I'll print some copies for you. We have waterproof paper. It's time to start. Do you have dance shoes?"

Sarah froze. *Dance shoes!*

"Oh no, I didn't think about it."

"You came to a dance class without dance shoes?" Diego raised his voice and looked at her. All the students stopped talking and stared.

"I'm sorry, it's just that... well, I didn't think to..." Sarah's words trailed off, her apology a mix of embarrassment and haste.

A hand slapped Diego's head from behind.

"You stop messing with her. She thinks you are serious," Maria's head popped from behind Diego, and a ripple of laughter broke out among the class. "Come here, darling," she wrapped her arms around her, giving her a big hug, "Shoes are great, but in tango, you just need an embrace. I'll keep an eye on his shenanigans." She looked at Diego, a full head and a half taller than her, and pointed her finger. "Don't you have a lesson to teach, you?"

Diego grinned mischievously at Sarah, rubbing the back of his head. He then lifted his shoulders and walked to the front of the room, in front of a mirror covering the entire wall. Sarah smiled at Maria and went to the back of the room, behind everyone else.

18

"Beginners in the front, advanced at the back. The less you know, the better you need to be able to see me," Diego said with friendly authority and pulled his mobile out of his pocket. With a click, a sultry tango melody filled the room, its rhythm pulsating through the air. "Everyone, zero position, changes of weight. Sarah, just mimic what you see. I'll help you in a while." He turned toward the mirror so that everyone could see his back.

Somehow, he looked taller when he was ready to dance. He lifted his left hand to his side at shoulder height, with his elbow bent. His right hand extended gracefully forward, in front of his sternum, as if he was embracing someone. His feet were touching each other. He gently shifted his weight from one leg to the other, each movement in perfect harmony with the music's rhythm.

Sarah lifted her left hand to her side, pretended to embrace someone with her right arm, and straightened her back. She changed her weight a few times left and right, but she was always a bit out of sync with the rest of the group. Sarah closed her eyes to concentrate on the rhythm. At that moment, she remembered how it felt when Diego made her change her weight in his embrace the previous night. Somehow, this made everything easier. *Breathe, left, right, left, right.* She smiled as she realized she was able to change weight following the music.

"Everyone, continue," Diego said and approached Sarah. "The leaders embrace with the right arm, the followers with the left." Sarah nodded, focused on the music. "Please use your *other* left arm to embrace," Diego whispered to her with a gentle chuckle.

Sarah glanced at her hands, a burst of laughter escaping her as she realized her mix-up. "I am sorry, I was focused on the music. I didn't want to miss the beat," she said, feeling like a 5-year-old girl who couldn't tell left from right.

Diego looked her in the eyes and smiled. "Tango waits. No need to run."

Sarah took an imaginary notepad and pretended she was taking notes. "Don't run behind men, trains, tango, and the beat. Noted."

"Everyone, find a partner," Diego said. Sarah surveyed the room, noticing couples forming. She spotted a lone figure and began

19

walking towards him. Diego's hand gently grasped hers. "Wait. Let him come to you." As if choreographed, the man noticed Sarah and crossed the room.

"Pablo, you started two years ago if I remember correctly," Diego said. Pablo nodded in agreement. "Please help Sarah. Sarah, he is going to walk forwards. You will be looking toward him. This means that you'll have to walk backward. Does it make sense?" Sarah nodded. "OK, everyone, let's hug and walk."

Pablo offered his embrace. "I guess this is when we hug," Sarah said, giving an awkward smile. She hesitated for a moment, Mark's words from last night echoing in her mind. Then she remembered the video. She took a step forward, placing her left hand on the back of his neck, with her elbow gently touching his right shoulder. Slowly, she lifted her right hand. Closing her eyes, she felt his right hand go around her. Pablo inhaled deeply, steadying himself, and Sarah, feeling his rhythmic breaths, synchronized her own breathing to match his. He took one step forward, and Sarah stepped backward. They paused, breathed again, and continued walking around the dance floor, step after step, breath after breath, until the song ended. Sarah opened her eyes.

"Wow. Where did you learn to embrace like that?" Pablo asked, smiling at her.

Sarah wasn't sure how to respond, but Diego's voice interrupted her thoughts. "Change partners!"

Sarah stayed where she was, and Diego approached her the moment the next song started. He offered his embrace.

Without hesitation, Sarah reached out, her left hand finding its place at the back of Diego's neck. Closing her eyes, she brought her body closer to his, taking a deep breath. Surprisingly, she felt Diego synchronizing his breath with hers. *It works both ways*, she realized. They walked together, hugging, for a whole song. When the song ended, Diego asked everyone to change partners again, but he stayed with her.

"Pablo asked me where I learned to embrace the way I do. Do you know what he meant?" Sarah asked.

20

"I think it's best if you discover the answer on your own," Diego replied with a smile. "Let's dance."

For the remainder of the class, Diego alternated between solo exercises for balance, changes of weight, turns, and dancing in couples. He dedicated time to correcting each student, adjusting their hand positions, posture, and hips. Though he approached Sarah multiple times, his focus remained on correcting her partners.

"How was the class?" Diego asked once the class ended.

"I enjoyed it. But," she hesitated as Diego looked directly into her eyes. Uncertain of how honest she could be, she glanced at some students that were still dancing.

"But," Diego repeated and stood beside her.

"But, you spent a lot of time correcting my partners and very little correcting me. Were you afraid you'd scare me away?"

Diego smiled. "Look at the women. What do you notice?"

Sarah observed each one, noting their graceful movements and steps. "They all dance very nicely," she remarked.

"What about their eyes?" Diego insisted.

"Nothing is wrong with their eyes," she responded, puzzled.

Diego took her hand and pulled her away from the other students. Speaking in a low voice, he said, "For most women, it takes weeks to trust their partners enough to close their eyes while dancing. Some take months or even years. It's not easy to trust a stranger, especially if that stranger doesn't really know what he is doing. It takes strength to let go and allow someone to lead you. It's much easier to put up a shield and stay in control. But you... You closed your eyes during the first song and every song after it. You hugged and trusted them."

Sarah looked at the dance floor. Almost every woman there danced with her eyes open.

"What about their left hands?" Diego asked.

Sarah looked and immediately felt her face turn red. Not a single one had her hand on the neck of their partners. They all placed their hands on their shoulder blades.

21

"I saw a video last night. She closed her eyes and put her hand on his neck. I thought that's how it should be. Oh gosh. Why didn't you say anything?"

Diego smiled. "Why don't you stay for the intermediate class?"

Sarah looked at him. "Are you messing with me again?"

Diego silently embraced her as the next song started. Sarah's left hand tentatively found its place on Diego's shoulder blade, her eyes remaining wide open, taking in every detail. Diego walked, changing his weight and stepping sometimes with the left foot and sometimes with the right. Sarah was confused, unsure which foot to use, and could no longer feel when she had to change her weight. Her gaze dropped to his feet, attempting to anticipate his movements and match his shifting weight in time. After an eternity that seemed to stretch on, Diego finally halted, marking an end to the confusing dance.

Sarah took a step back and looked at him. "I think I forgot everything you taught us today."

"Can you pinpoint what threw you off?" Diego asked.

"You kept changing your weight, and I wasn't fast enough to change my weight with you and step with the correct foot."

"What my feet do has nothing to do with what your feet need to do. I didn't lead a single change of weight, and yet you did thirty of them. Your eyes didn't help you. They confused you. You stopped feeling, you just analyzed. Now try it your way."

Sarah took a deep breath. She stepped forward and embraced him, placing her hand on the back of his neck and closing her eyes. The music started, but Diego didn't move. Sarah felt his right hand softly touching her back, and then she noticed something new. The middle of his chest became concave, as if he opened a space there for her. She took another deep breath, letting her chest fill that space. They exhaled together and started walking, step after step, breathing in unison. As Sarah subtly shifted her hand up Diego's neck, he responded in kind, his hand gliding slightly higher along her back, mirroring her movement in a silent dance of mutual adjustment. As he tightened the embrace, Sarah did too. *What's that feeling?* She thought. The scent of Diego's neck, a subtle hint of sandalwood, drifted to Sarah. As she exhaled, a faint shiver seemed to pass through Diego. *Did I just blow air on his neck?* The song ended, and they stayed hugging for a few seconds, breathing slowly.

She opened her eyes, and the sight of someone behind Diego jolted her back to reality, prompting her to instinctively step back, breaking their embrace. He looked at her, confused. Then he turned as he noticed a shade of red on the far side of the room. The woman who had been giving the classes with him the previous day was on the other side, staring at them.

"Jessica, you've made it! Excellent timing," Diego's voice rose, perhaps a touch too eagerly. "Sarah, are you staying?"

Sarah wasn't certain what to do. She took her mobile out of her back pocket and her heart sank – six missed calls. A surge of guilt washed over her. *Crap.* "Sorry, I have to go," she said and went as fast as she could toward the door, avoiding Jessica's eyes.

Chapter 5

Sarah removed her key from her purse as she climbed the stairs leading to her house. She paused outside the door for a few seconds, allowing her heartbeat to slow down. Silently, she slid the key into the lock and opened the door. The sound of the TV in the living room shutting off greeted her.

Mark was there, seated, staring at the black screen. Sarah could only see his back, but she knew he could see her reflection. She walked closer, hesitating momentarily as she thought about placing her hands on his shoulders. Something felt off, so she walked around the couch. Mark looked up at her.

"Where were you? I got worried."

"I'm sorry, I was stuck at work again, I forgot to text you."

"It's OK. What happened?"

"One of the instruments was missing again. They forgot to put it in the bag." Mark looked at her, saying nothing. Sarah felt her face grow warm, so she quickly turned toward the mini bar.

"I need a drink. Do you want one?"

"Thanks, but no. I've already had dinner, and yours is in the kitchen. I'm going to bed."

Sarah exhaled a sigh of relief when she heard the bedroom door close. She ate her dinner slowly and took an extra-long bath. By the time she entered the bedroom, Mark was already asleep. She gently got under the covers, staying still for a moment when she felt Mark stir slightly. Once she was certain he was fully asleep, she relaxed and rested her head on the pillow.

As she lay in bed, Sarah's thoughts turned to tango. In her mind, she danced across the floor, her stress and worries melting away with each movement. Her chest rose with the rhythm, and for a moment, she imagined Diego's chest in front of her. Shaking off the thought, she opened her eyes and reached for Mark's hand. *Focus, Sarah.*

Waking up next to Mark, still asleep as usual, Sarah felt a sense of normalcy. Most days, she needed to be at the hospital by 8 am, so she would get up an hour earlier to have breakfast and avoid morning traffic. Today was no different. Silently, she got out of bed, grabbed her slippers and a dress, and tiptoed out of the bedroom. She dressed in the living room, grabbed her bag, and left.

At her local bakery, a large plastic loaf of bread, sliced in half with 'Open' displayed in green letters, hung above the entrance. The morning sun filtered through the windows, illuminating an array of tempting treats. Sarah joined the line, her eyes scanning the display. At the counter, she greeted the cheerful young girl at the register and ordered a freshly baked croissant, golden and flaky, with a side of rich, aromatic coffee. The scent of buttery pastries and freshly brewed coffee filled the air.

She took her bag to the car and drove to the hospital. The morning surgery was simple. All she had to do was prepare the instruments, sit, and wait. Bored, she opened her Instagram feed, scrolling for a few seconds before dismissing it. She then went on Chrome and typed 'tango podcasts,' discovering a small list. One, 'The Curious Tanguero,' caught her attention. She closed her eyes and began listening.

After the surgery, Sarah cleaned the instruments and left the personnel-only area. Walking down the corridor, she spotted Mark.

"What are you doing here?" she asked with a smile.

"I thought we could have lunch together. I arrived a bit early, so I stopped by Laura's office to say hi."

A chill ran down Sarah's spine. "That was nice of you," she replied, forcing a smile. "What do you have in mind? Italian?"

"Why don't we go to the Food Market? That way, you can choose *whatever you prefer*." He emphasized the last three words, looking directly at her.

"Are you OK? You look strange," she whispered, placing her right hand on his cheek, a gesture she knew always calmed him. He looked at her and exhaled, closing his eyes.

"Laura told me you weren't working last night. Where were you?"

"I'm sorry," Sarah's voice trembled slightly. "Can we go outside? I need to tell you something." She saw the worry in Mark's eyes and felt a pang of guilt. "It's nothing important, just... silly, really."

25

They crossed the street in silence, entering a nearby park. The centerpiece was a serene, crystal-clear lake, where visitors strolled along winding paths. Lush, green lawns beckoned for picnics and sunbathing, and the gentle rustling of leaves provided a soothing soundtrack.

Sarah glanced at Mark, who seemed lost in his own contemplation, and her heart ached. She took Mark's hands in hers and looked up at him, unable to discern whether he was angry, sad, or something else.

"It's stupid. I wanted to tell you the other day about the tango class. I wanted to go. But then you started saying all those things about men who let their wives dance tango, and... And I didn't tell you. I'm sorry. I went to the class."

Mark stared at her in disbelief. "That's it? You went to a tango class?"

Sarah nodded.

"I thought..." Mark's voice trailed off, his eyes reflecting a mix of pain and relief, "you were seeing someone else."

Sarah felt a stab of guilt. "No, Mark, never. It's just... There's something about tango that draws me in, and I thought you wouldn't understand," she whispered.

"Look, I don't appreciate that you hid it from me. I understand it, but I don't like it. You lied to me. And for what? A tango class? How could a tango class be a good enough reason for you to lie?"

Sarah didn't respond. They stood in silence for a few minutes, staring at the lake.

Mark finally spoke. "I want you to be happy. I want us to be happy. *Together*. What's the point in seeking happiness outside of us? I know it might be fun to go out and dance all night with strangers, but that's not what our relationship is about. We are together. So let's be happy together." He put his hands around her shoulders and gazed into her eyes. "Forget about tango, you don't need it. I care about you. Let's go somewhere nice tonight."

Sarah nodded. "I'd like that," she replied, hugging him. *He cares, you stupid*, she thought. She tried to adjust her embrace to find his chest more comfortably, but he stepped back.

26

"Let's go, I know just the right place," he said.

Ten minutes later, they entered a restaurant. The rich, smoky aroma of grilled meats from the open kitchen greeted them. The brick walls, wooden beams, and dim, sultry lighting created an inviting atmosphere. Diners were engaged in animated conversations.

Sarah looked at the menu, featuring succulent cuts of beef, grilled to perfection and served with chimichurri sauce, alongside empanadas with various fillings. The wine list boasted a selection of Malbecs. However, what caught Sarah's attention was the name of the restaurant at the top of the menu. *La Cumparsita*. She shifted uncomfortably in her chair.

"Are you sure this is the right place?" she asked.

"It seems appropriate," Mark smiled and flagged down the waiter. "You wanted tango, I got you something better. Argentinian food."

The waiter, dressed in a crisp white shirt, black trousers, and a black apron, noticed them from across the room. He approached gracefully, skillfully navigating around other waiters carrying trays of sizzling meats and delicious empanadas.

"Hola chicos, what can I bring you?" he asked with a broad smile.

"We'll start with empanadas, one with tender beef and the other with a medley of vegetables. What's the chimichurri sauce?"

"Chimichurri is the magic potion of Argentina! It's as lively as a tango and as bold as a soccer match! We start with vibrant green parsley, just like the lush fields of the Pampas. Then, we add a generous amount of garlic cloves. Next, we mix in red wine vinegar, a dash of fiery red pepper flakes for a sizzle, and a touch of oregano for that herbal twist. We finish it off with the finest olive oil for a little luxury, and don't forget a sprinkle of salt and pepper for the final flavor fiesta! Now, let's whisk it all together with a smile as wide as the Rio de la Plata, and voila! Our secret sauce that's as bold as an Argentinean heart and as irresistible as our empanadas! Buen provecho!"

Mark and Sarah exchanged a look and laughed.

"That was amazing!" Mark said to the waiter, who gave an elegant bow in response. "I told you," Mark smiled at Sarah, "I know just the right place."

Mark ordered an Argentine steak, cooked on the open grill and accompanied by a side of garlic mashed potatoes and grilled vegetables. To complement their meal, he selected a robust bottle of Malbec. "Thank you," said Sarah. "Together," responded Mark, holding her hand. "Together is always better."

Sarah took a moment to observe the walls. On one, she saw a large, weathered map of Argentina, marking the regions and provinces of the country. Surrounding it was an assortment of vintage framed photographs showcasing tango dancers and soccer players. Sarah could only recognize Maradona. She also noticed a shelf with a small, roundish cup made of a natural, wood-like material. Its surface had an earthy, rustic texture and was decorated with colorful, intricate patterns. A straw-like object protruded from the top.

Next to it was a musical instrument resembling an accordion, but larger. Parts of it looked like folded leather, adorned with intricate designs. On the front of the instrument, there were hundreds of buttons. Beneath it, in black letters on a small golden sign, read two words: *El Bandoneon*.

However, what caught her attention was another wall. It was completely empty except for one framed picture in the middle and an old turntable for vinyl records in front of it. In the photo, there was the face of a man with a radiant smile. His happiness seemed genuine, not just a smile of the lips, but one that reached his eyes. "Who is this one?" she asked the waiter as he delivered the empanadas.

"You don't know who that is?" The waiter looked at her with exaggerated surprise. "That's Carlos Gardel! Come with me," he said and moved toward the wall.

Sarah looked at Mark, who nodded in approval. She followed the waiter.

"Picture this. It's the early twentieth century in the lively streets of Buenos Aires. Gardel, a charming man with a voice that could make hearts skip a beat, is belting out tangos in the smoky bars of the city.

Legend has it that he was born in France, but we've claimed him as our own. He became the most beloved tango crooner of his time, and his songs? They're like the love stories of the city itself. Gardel took tango from the back alleys to the grand theaters, and he didn't just sing. He practically oozed charisma. His slicked-back hair, sharp suits, and that smile that could melt glaciers... it drove the ladies wild! When you listen to Gardel's music, you're not just hearing tango. You're experiencing the very soul of Buenos Aires. Wait."

With a playful smile, the waiter carefully selected a vinyl record from a collection next to the wall. He treated it as if it were a precious artifact. "Carlos Gardel," he announced with a flourish. Approaching the turntable, he inspected the vinyl, gently wiping away a bit of dust with a quick blow. Holding it up to the light, he showed Sarah that the record was ready. With a theatrical spin, he centered the vinyl on the turntable's platter. Making eye contact with Sarah, he smiled and whispered, "The pièce de résistance." He carefully lowered the stylus onto the record. As the needle gently touched down, he glanced around playfully, noting a few curious looks from nearby diners. As the first notes of tango music filled the restaurant, the waiter stepped back, hands on his hips, nodding to the rhythm. Some diners started tapping their feet. He leaned toward Sarah. "The song is called 'Mi Buenos Aires Querido.' My beloved Buenos Aires. Do you dance?"

Sarah glanced at Mark, then back at the waiter, her expression a mix of nostalgia and restraint.

"Don't worry, I understand," the waiter winked.

"Thank you," Sarah smiled. "I'll go back now." She took a few steps forward, then paused. Though she couldn't understand the lyrics, there was something in Gardel's voice that stirred a deep longing within her. Taking a deep breath, she walked toward her table with a calm, rhythmic stride. A warm feeling spread through her chest. Arriving at the table, she collected her feet together. *Zero position,* she thought and sat down.

"Don't let your empanada get cold," Mark said. "It's amazing."

Sarah smiled. "I won't."

I won't.

29

Chapter 6

"Hey, are you in the studio?" Sarah asked as she placed her headphones on.

"On my way there, planning to practice a bit. Everything OK?" Diego responded.

"Listen, a surgery got canceled, and I have a couple of hours free. Do you give private classes? I could be there in 20 minutes. It's hard for me to come to the afternoon class," she said, glancing at her locker.

"Sure, chica, come over."

She removed her scrubs and left the hospital. Her face beamed with a radiant smile as she slipped into the driver's seat. She connected her mobile's Bluetooth, and soon Gardel's voice filled the car, her fingers tapping rhythmically on the wheel.

"What is this music?" a young parking attendant asked while validating her ticket. "It sounds like it's from the eighties."

"You are a couple of years off," Sarah smiled. "I think it's from the twenties."

"I've been listening to the radio all day, every day, miss. This song isn't new," he laughed.

"Different twenties," Sarah smiled. "See you tomorrow."

When she arrived at the studio, most of the lights were off, and a thin beam of light passed through a crack in the window, hitting the dance floor. Diego's back was to her as he stood in front of the mirror. He wore black trousers and a crisp, snow-white dress shirt with sleeves rolled up to his elbows. His black leather dance shoes gleamed under the dim light, reflecting the muted chandeliers overhead. There was no music, but Sarah could hear him breathing. With each breath, his chest rose and fell, his arms embracing an imaginary partner.

A few seconds later, he began to move, tracing intricate patterns on the floor. Each step, each rotation, each elegant flick of his foot was done with precision. It looked effortless, as if he had done them thousands of times before. The room was silent, except for the echo of his shoes on the hardwood. Whispering footsteps, sensual swishes, gentle murmurs – each step had its own sound. Every time he moved close to the ray of light, Sarah noticed dust swirling in the air. As he executed a series of quick footwork, his legs became a blur of motion. His movement oscillated, sometimes intense and fast, and other times calm and almost motionless, as if he were listening to a rhythm that no one else could hear.

Sarah shifted her gaze to his reflection in the mirror. Her eyebrows lifted as she realized his eyes were closed. He had a serene smile on his face as he continued dancing, no matter how fast he moved. In the gentle glow of the room, his features looked relaxed, the lines of his face soft. Only his eyelids moved every now and then, as if his eyes were looking left and right underneath.

The sound of the steps faded as he came to a stop, precisely at the same spot where he had begun, feet together. He took a few deep breaths, opened his eyes, and gazed directly at his reflection.

Sarah waited until she saw his body relax.

He looked at her, and his smile broadened. "When did you sneak in?"

"I think it was at the beginning of your imaginary song," Sarah confessed, realizing she probably should have let him know she was there earlier.

"It's not imaginary. It's called *El huracan*, the hurricane." Diego approached her and gave her a hug.

"Do you have tiny earbuds?" Sarah laughed, turning his head to the side and looking at his ears. "Because I didn't hear anything."

"I know this song too well for my own good," he responded, and Sarah noticed a cloud over his eyes.

"What is it about?"

"You don't want to know," Diego said with a smile, shifting into teacher mode. "So, what do you want to learn?"

Sarah took a moment. She hadn't had time to think about it. "I guess I assumed you would know," she said.

"I know *my* path, Sarah. I don't know *yours*. What is it that *you* want?"

32

Sarah looked at the ceiling for a few moments. "I want," she hesitated. "I want to learn how to dance... Better than Jessica."

Diego's eyes widened, and his head moved back for a fraction of a second. Then he burst into laughter, covering his face with his hands.

She felt her face getting red again. "Hey! Stop it! It's not funny."

Diego lifted his hands and showed her his palms as a sign of surrender. "I am sorry. You are right."

"You don't think I can, do you?" she challenged, a hint of accusation in her voice.

Diego remained silent for a few seconds.

"Never mind, I think I'll just go home. Sorry to bother you," Sarah said, turning to leave.

Diego moved quickly, blocking her path. She stopped a breath apart from him but didn't move back, just looking him in the eyes. Her arms hung straight down, and with a sudden burst of emotion, she clenched her fists tightly. "You don't think I can."

"It's not that I think you can't," Diego whispered. "I think you are setting the bar too low."

Sarah took a few seconds to realize what Diego had said. She closed her eyes, took a deep breath, and then released it as a tear ran down her cheek. "I want it. I don't know why, I don't know how. But I want it."

Diego put his right arm around her back, and with his left, he gently pulled her head closer. Sarah placed her forehead on his shoulder as more tears started flowing. She began shaking. "I want it." Diego gently placed her hand on his chest, and she turned, her cheek brushing against his. She sensed that familiar change of weight and followed. Left, right, left, right. Diego breathed, and they started walking. His embrace felt soft, comfortable. *What's that feeling?* Sarah felt her shivering gradually calming. Step by step, she moved. Her left hand went all the way around Diego's neck until her fingers felt the back of his ear. Diego responded by creating that space inside his embrace, a space that drew Sarah right in. She allowed herself to melt in there. Another step. *What's that feeling?* She could hear the sound of their feet sliding above the floor, caressing it.

Diego rotated his chest, and Sarah felt her chest rotating too. He changed the direction of the movement, and little by little, the steps became more complicated. Sarah found herself rotating, accelerating, leaning forward. Yet, Diego's embrace never stopped being soft and gentle. Everything seemed so clear. She could feel his feet pushing the floor, moving them both, as one, to the next step. *What's that feeling?* Diego slowed down. They took their last steps and came to a halt. Diego didn't make any move to release the embrace, and neither did Sarah. They breathed together. Sarah let a bit more of her weight fall on him and put her forehead on his shoulder again. He squeezed her hand on his chest. *Home.*

They stayed like this until Sarah lost track of time. *How long can an embrace last before it's considered cheating?* she thought. But time passed, and she stayed there, waiting.

"They warned me not to wear white shirts in tango. They become transparent when women cry on them," Diego said playfully a few minutes later.

Drying her eyes with her hand, Sarah teased, "You got a lot of them crying on you?"

"No, you are the first," Diego said.

Sarah nodded.

"Well, for today," Diego continued with a big grin on his face.

"You are a goof, you know that?" Sarah said and pushed him back playfully.

"That's why I am happy. You should try it sometimes."

"Am I paying for this invaluable tango advice?"

"I don't think you can afford it. So, let's try something cheaper. Show me how you pivot."

"How I *what* now?"

"A pivot is the rotative movement of your foot in relation to the floor. Imagine you are hugging a partner in front of you. Put your feet together. Allow the back of your feet to touch each other. Now, put all your weight on your right foot. Can you lift your left foot in the air?"

Sarah nodded.

"If you can lift your left leg in the air, that means all your weight is on the right foot. That's what you need. Your right foot is now the base leg. Now, put most of your weight on the front of the right foot, and then rotate it, any direction you want."

Sarah rotated her right foot toward the left.

"Now look at the mirror."

Sarah observed herself. The right foot was pointing toward the left corner of the room.

"Where are your hips pointing?" Diego asked.

"To the left corner."

"And where is your chest pointing?"

"The same."

"And where is your partner?" he said, his mischievous smile returning.

"I guess he is where I left him?"

"Then why is your chest looking toward the left and not at him?"

Sarah took a moment to think. A second later, she rotated her chest toward the front of the room.

Diego nodded and smiled. "Your legs can move independently while your upper body stays connected with your partner. There is no need to leave him behind when you change your direction."

Sarah nodded and tried a few pivots. "I did pivots many times when we danced, right?"

"Yes."

"If I can already do them, why are you teaching them to me now?"

Diego leaned closer. "There is a difference between doing something without understanding it and doing it while knowing what you are doing. You won't notice it at the beginning of your learning journey, but it will become clear later. If you understand how something works, you can modify it later and improve it. If not, you are stuck with it. When it comes to your pivot, what do you do with your body to create it?"

Sarah looked at the mirror and tried a few times. She noticed her chest rotating, then the hips, then the feet.

Where is your partner? She asked herself. She tried again, this time keeping her chest forward and starting the rotation from the hips.

35

"You see?" Diego said. "Your pivot started from a different point now. Can you initiate it directly from your foot?"

Sarah attempted a few times.

"Can you take a step back after the pivot?" asked Diego.

Sarah executed a pivot and stepped back.

"This is an *ocho*. Try starting the pivot from the chest, or from the hips, or from the foot," Diego instructed.

Sarah made several attempts. "What's the right way?" she eventually asked.

"Welcome to the world of tango," Diego responded, extending his arm gracefully and taking a bow. "I'll share how I see it and what works for me. Other teachers will tell you something different. I almost never think of the pivot. I focus solely on the result I want to achieve. Why do we pivot?"

"To change direction?" Sarah ventured.

"Yes, changing direction is one use of a pivot. Imagine you're about to cross a street, listening to 'Fueron Tres Años' on your headphones."

"I know this song," Sarah said proudly, remembering that first video she watched a few days ago.

"You step onto the street and see a car approaching from the right. Now, if you value your life, what do you do?"

"I stop?"

"In the middle of the street? Do you want to die? Well, sometimes that song has that effect on people," he chuckled.

Sarah laughed.

"But no, you don't stop. You jump back. And if you value your life, you jump back *and* diagonally to the left, since the car is coming from your right. Now, you could do it in two ways. You pivot to change your direction, and then you push off the street to move your body back. But no one does it this way. When you see the car, you jump away. Your pivot and the change of direction happen together after you push with your base leg. You push the street forward and to the right, so you can jump back and to the left. Do you understand?"

Sarah wasn't entirely sure.

"The pivot happens *because* of the push," Diego clarified, "not before. Give it a try. Legs together. All your weight on the left foot. Now, make a step backward and diagonally to the left. Focus on pushing the floor forward and diagonally to the right. This will take you in the opposite direction. Forget about the pivot. Just push the floor."

Sarah tried the movement with each leg. "It's easier that way," she remarked.

"One last thing. Move in any direction, but don't focus on where you want to go. Inhale, and as you exhale, focus on pushing the floor toward the opposite direction."

Sarah took a step to the right.

"Push," Diego instructed.

She inhaled and took a step diagonally forward.

"Push," he repeated.

She pushed herself toward a back step.

"Push!"

Sarah looked at him. "Breathe, push, breathe, push... I feel like I'm about to give birth."

Diego smiled. "Maybe you are."

He took his phone from his pocket, and a few seconds later, a song started. The notes were not as soft as in other tango songs Sarah had heard. They resembled a soundtrack to a dramatic love story approaching its crucial conflict. "It's called Emancipacion. The orchestra is Osvaldo Pugliese. Let's walk."

Diego's embrace felt different this time. His muscles were tense, and his left elbow pointed toward the floor. Sarah felt his ribcage closing. She mirrored him, her weight shifting to the front of her right foot as Diego took a tiny step back. Then something shifted. Diego pushed the floor with strength, accelerating her entire body backward. Each step was a small explosion, followed by a brief moment of calmness until the next explosion.

"Push," Diego whispered.

Sarah didn't hesitate. She concentrated on pushing herself back as Diego stepped forward, right where her foot had been a fraction of a second ago. Step after step, she grasped the sensation of a genuine push. Her ribcage stayed contracted, and her muscles remained tense.

"Breathe," Diego said, pausing as the music slowed down.

Sarah allowed the air to fill her lungs and adjusted her hand on his neck.

"And push!"

But Sarah didn't need the warning. She was ready for it. The music had prepared her. Step by step, she tuned into the melody's shifts, how it slowed, then quickened, and how the beat momentarily vanished before resurging with greater intensity. They synchronized their muscles, tightening and then melting into each other's embrace. They inhaled deeply and then rapidly. The music picked up pace one final time before reaching its conclusion.

Sarah sensed her breath gradually calming, her body unwinding into a state of bliss. She had experienced this bliss before. Her face reddened as she realized when.

Diego loosened the embrace and took a step back. "I told you, you were setting the bar too low," he remarked.

Sarah smiled. I am good at this.

Chapter 7

"Where are you going?" Mark asked, glancing up briefly from the game. The entire living room was bathed in an otherworldly greenish hue, a result of the 146-inch TV illuminating the space during a football game.

"I'm meeting Linda for a couple of drinks," Sarah replied, grabbing her coat.

"Who's Linda?" Mark brought a slice of pizza to his nose and inhaled deeply.

"You haven't met her yet," Sarah said. "Would you like to join us?" Mark gestured with his pizza slice towards the TV. "I'd love to meet her sometime, but you know how I get with these games. Rain check?" He stood up and gave Sarah a hug. "Enjoy your night!"

After waving goodbye to Mark, Sarah stepped outside, the cool night air a stark contrast to the warmth of their living room. She settled into her car and set her destination in Google Maps, her mood lifting as the first notes of a tango playlist filled the car, syncing rhythmically with the digital voice guiding her.

There should be a Google Maps app for tango steps, Sarah thought wistfully as she extended her hand out the window, waiting at a traffic light. "Turn. Right. Here. Turn. Right. Here. Crap. Recalculating. Embrace again," she mimicked the voice, laughing. For the rest of the ride, Sarah tapped her fingers on the wheel, envisioning how she would dance to each of the songs. Song after song, she pondered the possibilities, contemplating moments when she would adjust the embrace, making it either softer or more intense. As she turned the steering wheel to align with the angled parking spaces, a warm sensation washed over her chest. She waited for the final song to conclude, all the while observing people carrying shopping bags as they walked along the sidewalk.

"So, you're the one Diego keeps talking about," a woman's voice echoed through the intercom. "Come up, first floor, the one with the dancing couple on the front."

Ascending the stairs, Sarah was greeted by a smiling woman who embraced her warmly. "Tango people really know how to embrace," said Sarah. "Nice to meet you, Linda."

"Practice makes perfect," Linda replied with a smile. "Come inside."

Linda's vibrant presence was complemented by her striking appearance. In her mid-forties, with a graceful, athletic build, her auburn hair cascaded in loose waves around her face. Her eyes sparkled with energy, and she wore a flowing dress and high heels. Sarah stared at them for a few seconds.

"These just arrived. I was testing them," Linda said, removing her heels and handing them to Sarah. "Sit here. Try them on. You wear a size 36, right?"

"You're good," Sarah responded.

"It's my job, honey. Of course, I'm good. The mirror is to your right," Linda said, clicking on a tiny MP3 player. Soft tango notes filled the room. "I'll be back with tea in a minute."

The heels, a rich, verdant color with a design like intricate flower petals, felt soft and velvety under Sarah's touch, with a subtle give that promised comfort.

Sarah removed her right shoe and held one of these little green pieces of heaven in front of her for a few seconds, as if savoring that feeling of excitement and anticipation. The initial touch of the smooth material against her skin was gentle. She fastened the straps and examined herself in the mirror. Her leg appeared longer. She stood up and viewed herself from the side. She wondered what Mark would say if he saw her now in these heels.

"That tanguera looks gooooood," Linda commented, returning with tea.

Sarah looked confused.

"A tanguera is a woman who dances tango," Linda explained. "Notice how supportive they are around your ankle?"

"They're unlike any heels I've worn before," Sarah marveled. "So comfortable."

"Many tangueras wear them to work. If they're good for dancing for hours, they're great for the office," Linda added.

Sarah imagined the reaction of the doctors as she walked through the hospital hallways in her green heels and baggy green scrubs. "What, you've never seen a walking plant?" she would say.

"They are beautiful. How much do they cost?" she asked.

"Not so fast, honey," Linda said. "You don't marry the first man you date, do you? You need to make sure everything fits. How many dresses do you have that match this color?"

Sarah lifted her hand, forming a circle by bringing the top of her index finger to meet her thumb.

"That's what I thought," Linda smiled. "Now, you can either buy a few dresses to match the shoes, or you can do what every smart tanguera does." She stood up and moved toward the wall on the left. With a theatrical flair, Linda pointed at a blue button on the right.

Sarah looked at the button, confused. Then she looked at the wall. *This isn't a wall. It's a closet.*

"Will you do the honor?" Linda smiled.

Sarah jumped off the couch, one foot in heels, one in sneakers, and pressed the button. The closet doors gracefully slid open, making a soft, hushed sound, revealing a walk-in closet. The integrated LED lighting gently illuminated the meticulously arranged contents. Sarah was astounded.

"These are..."

"A hundred and twenty-three pairs of tango shoes for you to choose from," Linda announced.

Sarah's mouth fell open. She walked in and looked around. All the shoes were arranged by color, creating a canvas of elegance. "Where do I start?"

"First, black. Then, red," Linda said, waving two pairs of heels in front of Sarah's face with a huge grin.

Sarah tried on several pairs, each one more enticing than the last, her excitement growing with every fit. "Linda, this has been amazing, but I feel like I'm taking too much of your time," Sarah said after a while.

"I remember buying my first tango shoes," Linda reminisced. "I'm just happy to be part of your journey. So, where do we stand?"

41

Sarah pointed at three pairs of high heels in front of her, each accompanied by an elegant iridescent lilac shoe bag.

Linda looked at them. "A classic black, a deep red, and... what do we have here?" she smiled at Sarah, lifting the third pair. "Tiger-patterned leather. The lace-up design cinches around the foot, with black suede also adorned with tiger-stripe leather accents. Are you buying these for the dance floor or the bedroom?"

"Sometimes, I can't tell the difference," Sarah smiled.

Linda looked at her. "He dances well, doesn't he?"

"It makes you wonder," Sarah replied, a blush creeping into her cheeks.

Linda picked up the red shoes and placed them next to Sarah's face. "Yep, these ones fit."

Sarah laughed. "Please don't say anything, OK?"

"Oh honey, I don't think it would make any difference. The embrace doesn't lie. Trust me, I've had many of those. And speaking of which, how about we take these out for a spin? There's a milonga five minutes from here. They should be starting now."

"What's a milonga?"

Linda looked at her, surprised. "Does Diego ever explain anything in that class, or are you just hugging and walking? Now, you don't happen to have a dress with you, do you? Mistake number one. Always have a dress and a pair of shoes in the car. You never know when you'll need them. Come with me."

Linda led Sarah to a nearby room and opened another closet. Sarah's mouth dropped open at the sight. Tens of tango dresses, arranged by color from black to purple, yellow, and even white, were on display. There was even one that appeared semi-transparent.

"I didn't know you sold dresses too. Maybe I'll get those green heels after all," Sarah said.

Linda smiled. "Honey, I have to confess something. These aren't for sale."

Sarah's eyes widened. "Yours?"

Linda nodded. "My name is Linda, and I am a dress-a-holic. I have even more at my home. Now, try this on. It goes with your black heels."

Sarah took the dress in her hands. It was a red tango dress with a low-cut neckline and an asymmetrical hemline, slightly longer at the back. The back also featured a daring low-cut design, which made Sarah smile. "Are you trying to sell me too?" she joked without taking her eyes off the dress. "Where can I change?"

"Uhhh... here?" Linda suggested.

When Sarah looked away from the dress, she realized Linda was right behind her, dressed only in underwear and a bra. She turned her head the other way.

"I'll wear a black dress and red shoes. We'll be a hit," Linda said. "Do you need makeup?"

"Where are we going again?" Sarah asked.

"We're going dancing. I'll explain everything when we get to the milonga," Linda said.

Chapter 8

Sarah's phone rang as they were parking the car. "It's Mark, my boyfriend," she said.

Linda gave her a teasing, raised-eyebrow look and a cheeky smile. "You have a boyfriend?"

"Now you be quiet. He doesn't know I dance tango," Sarah whispered.

"Hey, how was the game?" Sarah asked Mark.

"I'm pretty sure the referee's favorite color is yellow, given all the cards he handed out tonight. It was a mess. Are you enjoying your drinks?"

"It's fun, I'm here with Linda. I've put you on speakerphone. Linda, say hi."

"Heeeeyyyy," Linda chimed in. "No drinks yet, we've only had tea."

"Now that's a friend I can get used to," Mark said cheerfully. "Linda, I'd love to have you over sometime. Pumpkin, I'm heading to bed. Just wanted to say goodnight."

Linda made a heart shape with her hands and Sarah playfully punched her on the shoulder.

"OK, I'll try not to wake you. See you tomorrow." Sarah hung up the phone.

"So, what's his story?" Linda inquired.

"We've been together for five years. He's handsome, has a great job, and even bought us a home. Without him, I don't think I could afford to stay in this city. He's wonderful," Sarah replied.

"That sounds serious. But where's the diamond?"

"No diamonds or kids yet," Sarah said. "He works long hours. There's no time for that."

"Are you planning to have kids?"

"Yes, we had planned to."

"When's the due date?"

"Three years ago," Sarah sighed.

"I see," Linda said. "How old are you?"

"Approaching the limit."

44

Sarah turned the car into a parking spot. "Forget about that now. We're here."

They were in a part of the city Sarah usually avoided. As they stepped out, a strong fishy odor hit them. Sarah glanced at the nearby garbage bins, swarming with flies. The area had an eerie feel, with elongated shadows stretching across the cobblestone path. A broken alleyway light dangled, its cables swinging. The sound of female voices cheering and shouting 'Good evening' to passing cars filled the air every few seconds.

"There's a fish market here in the mornings," Linda said. "Come on."

Sarah gave her car a last look, wondering if it was safe. As they walked, a homeless man appeared, stopping to stare at them. Sarah realized he was probably not used to seeing two women dressed elegantly in red and black walking this street at this hour of the night. His eyes looked at the pavement again, and Sarah saw him bend his knees and pick up a half-smoked cigarette. A smile appeared on his face.

"We're here," Linda announced, pressing a doorbell.

Inside, they headed to an elevator. Linda lifted a protective iron latch and pulled an ornate lever. The elevator hummed softly, its accordion gate unfolding to reveal intricate, old machinery. Linda closed the gate and pressed number seven. Sarah watched as each floor passed by.

After door number four, Sarah felt a vibration in her ear. When the little number '5' appeared in front of her, she listened to some muted notes. Door six, and the music became clearer. As the elevator decelerated, she also heard people chatting and laughing. Linda pulled the iron gate to the side and pushed the door open. Two women stood in the hallway.

"Hola guapa!" they greeted, hugging Linda.

"Ladies, this is Sarah. It's her first milonga," Linda introduced.

"Hey, I'm Carla, and this is Monica. Whatever you do, don't dance with the guy in red pants, or the one in sneakers, they'll drag you around. And avoid the guy with the hat. He thinks he's Gardel and won't stop singing. The rest are fine," Carla advised and Monica nodded in agreement.

45

"Red pants, sneakers, Gardel," Sarah repeated. "Thanks!"

"Sarah, this is Elli. It's her milonga."

Elli was seated next to a tiny desk by the entrance. About 30 years old and blond, she welcomed them with a big smile. She stood up and gave them both a long hug.

"This one is on me. You pay the next one," Linda smiled at Sarah, handing Elli some notes. "It's her first milonga. She is Diego's student."

"You came on the right night. Please keep the ticket to redeem it for one free drink," Elli said with a smile.

Sarah walked through the door and found herself already on the dance floor. A few couples were dancing underneath a slowly rotating disco ball.

"Let's go to that couch," Linda pointed toward a glass wall on the right side of the floor.

Sarah started crossing the dance floor when she felt Linda's arm on her back.

"Not *through* the dance floor, pumpkin, *around* it."

Sarah laughed. Only Mark used to call her pumpkin, but Linda could pull it off too. She looked outside the glass wall. From the seventh floor, she could see a large part of the city. She looked down and noticed her car too. *Still there, good.* To the right, she saw another street. About ten young women were there, probably not older than twenty, all dressed in tiny skirts. *They must be freezing.* A car approached, and they ran toward it, forcing it to slow down. They all started talking to the driver through the window. After a brief moment, the car accelerated again. The girls went back and sat on the stairs of a building entrance, waiting for the next car.

"Come sit with me," said Linda. "Time to take off those sneakers, don't you think?"

Sarah returned to the couch. She pulled out her black heels and looked at them. They sparkled every few moments as the disco ball rotated.

"So, how does this work?" she asked Linda once she was done.

"I am dancing this *tanda*. I'll explain everything after," Linda said and stood up as a fast and happy tango tune started. A man

46

appeared in perfect timing in front of her. She gave a nod to Sarah and stood in front of Linda. Sarah watched them dance elegantly across the dance floor. Linda's posture was very similar to Jessica's, but she was leaning forward significantly. It looked like she was hanging from her partner. Her left arm was positioned differently too. The inside part of her elbow was above his shoulder, and her arm extended all the way back to the middle of his back. Her fingers were spread as if she wanted to cover as much surface as possible.

His posture differed from Diego's too. He also leaned a bit forward, though not as much as Linda. His right arm wrapped completely around Linda's back, so much that his right hand managed to reach her ribcage on the opposite side.

They both had big smiles on their faces all the time. Sarah noticed that they didn't take large steps. Instead, they executed a lot of quick, small ones. They performed one combination, repeated it two or three times, then did another and repeated it.

When the song ended, they released their embrace, and chatted before embracing again.

Sarah noticed a guy behind them looking at her. Their eyes locked for a second, and he smiled at her, tilting his head. Sarah looked toward Linda again. She stared at her feet, moving fast, changing directions, pivoting, crossing. As they passed in front of the guy, Sarah noticed he was still looking at her. She turned her head to the left to avoid his gaze, only to realize another man was staring at her too. She decided to focus on Linda's feet. *No guys there.* When the third song ended, Sarah looked in disbelief as she heard the first notes of "I Disappear," her favorite song by Metallica. Linda and her partner walked toward the couch, with one arm wrapped around each other's backs and the other hand gesturing rock horns. The man nodded at Sarah and returned to his seat. "That was so much fun. I love to start the night with a milonga," Linda said and then turned toward the guy at the bar next to them. "Two glasses of red, please."

"So that's a milonga?" Sarah asked.

Linda smiled. "Milonga can mean different things. It can refer to this place, what you would call a tango party. But it can also mean a type of tango dance that's fast and happy."

"Diego didn't show me this," Sara said.

"You don't usually learn milonga in the first classes. It's hard to be fast and relaxed at the same time."

"Why are they playing Metallica?"

"That's called a cortina. It's just fifteen to twenty seconds of non-tango songs so that we know it's time to go back to our seats."

As if on cue, the DJ turned the volume down, and the melodic notes of a tango filled the room. Sarah looked up to see men walking around the floor, stopping in front of women who were already smiling at them. Then, she noticed a young man looking at her. He was dressed entirely in black, his form-fitting tuxedo jacket impeccably tailored to accentuate his physique, paired with a crisply pressed black dress shirt, slightly unbuttoned at the collar. His sleek black trousers hugged his legs with precision, elongating his frame, and a pair of black patent leather tango shoes gleamed under the disco light.

"There is a man staring at me," she whispered to Linda. "And there were two other men staring at me before, during your tamda."

Linda almost spilled her wine laughing. "It's called a 'tanda.' And he's not just staring; he's asking you to dance. Just look at him and smile."

"You mean flirt?"

"Just do it, I'll explain afterward."

Sarah felt her face redden as she turned toward the guy's direction. He was still looking at her, tilting his head slightly. Sarah smiled, and he immediately started walking toward her.

"Stay seated until he arrives," Linda advised.

He stopped in front of her, smiled at Linda, and offered his hand. Sarah placed her hand in his and stood up, feeling her legs shake a bit as her heart started to race.

His embrace felt different from Diego's. She felt his chest only on her left side, and his arms were less firm. Sarah took a deep breath and placed her hand on his neck. They started walking. She could understand what he wanted to do, but she didn't feel as certain as with Diego. Glancing behind his back, she saw Linda pointing her phone in their direction. *Great, that's what I needed, video proof.* At that moment, she felt her body falling to the side, out of balance. She tensed her hands, shaking the man's body to stabilize herself. He took a tiny step back, trying to find his balance. "I am sorry," she whispered, "I am a beginner." The man didn't respond but adjusted his embrace, hugging her softly. Sarah followed his breath and closed her eyes.

Everything became clearer with each breath. Sarah could feel his feet pushing the floor, making it easier to anticipate when his chest would rotate.

The first song ended, and Sarah waited with her eyes closed for him to release the embrace. He didn't. They danced three more songs, maintaining the embrace, until the cortina began. This time, it was a romantic ballad Sarah didn't recognize. She thanked the man and walked back to her seat.

She found herself thinking of Mark, wondering what he might think of this hidden world of tango she had discovered.

"You made this one very happy," Linda remarked.

"What do you mean?"

"Hand on the neck, four songs without breaking the embrace, your eyes closed, a calm walk. If I didn't know you, I'd think you've been dancing for at least five years. And now, *they* probably think so too."

They? Sarah lifted her head. Everywhere she looked, there were guys staring at her.

"What's happening?" she asked, barely containing her surprise.

"What's happening is that by the end of the night, you'll thank me for selling you these comfortable heels, pumpkin. You won't be sitting much tonight."

Chapter 9

"Did you go shopping yesterday?" Mark dangled one of the shoe bags in front of Sarah.

Sarah glanced at the bag. "Give a girl the right shoes, and she can conquer the world," she said, channeling her best Marilyn Monroe.

"Believe you can and you're halfway there," Mark replied in a strong, commanding voice.

"Who are you supposed to be?" Sarah asked.

"I was aiming for Theodore Roosevelt," Mark said, tilting his head to the side. "And how exactly are those shoes going to help you conquer the world?"

Sarah paused, unsure of how to respond. "Just joking. I saw them and felt like buying them. Do you want to see?"

"Sure. But aren't you going to show me the other ones too?" He nodded towards the couch behind her.

Surprised, Sarah turned and saw the other two pairs on the coffee table. "I went a bit crazy, didn't I?" she asked playfully.

"So, are these for work?" Mark's forehead creased slightly.

"I can wear them for many occasions. Why are you so interested in shoes all of a sudden?" She smiled, smoothing out a wrinkle on her sleeve.

"I'm actually more interested in the *bags*," he said, his smile fading and his brows knitting together. He handed her one of the bags and walked towards the kitchen.

"What do you mean?" Holding the bag, Sarah watched him walk away, then looked down. A cold shiver ran up her spine as she read the gold lettering in an elegant font. 'Tango Shoes For Life.'

She tossed the bag onto the couch and followed him into the kitchen. Mark stood there, teapot in one hand and cup in the other, pouring tea silently. Sarah watched him, unsure of what to say.

"I'm sorry," she finally said.

Mark set the teapot down. "Sorry for what?"

"I'm sorry I hid going back for another class."

"That's all?" His expression softened as he took a sip of tea.

50

Sarah hesitated, then confessed, "And I'm sorry I hid going out to dance."

"That's where you were yesterday?" Mark asked, taking a long sip.

Sarah nodded.

"You danced with your teacher?"

"No, he wasn't there," she replied, noticing his jaw tense.

"Then who did you dance with?" he asked, returning the cup to his lips.

"Just some guys, I don't even know their names."

Mark slammed the cup onto the table, the sound echoing in the room. Sarah stepped back as he looked up at her intently.

"So let me get this straight. You lie about the tango class, then you lie again, then you go dancing with random guys and lie about that too. Am I missing anything?"

"It's just dancing, Mark. Why don't you come with me next time? You'll see."

"The *next* time, huh? Does our relationship mean anything to you anymore?"

Sarah's lips pressed into a tight line. Slowly, her expression darkened. Her nostrils flared and her jaw tensed before she burst out, "What are you talking about? I told you. It's just a dance! What the hell does this have to do with us?"

Mark met her outburst with a few seconds of silence. Then, leaning in, his voice dropped to a low whisper, his gaze intensely fixed on hers. "If I were you, I would think well before taking this step," he advised, then turned and left the kitchen. Moments later, Sarah, still rooted to the spot, heard the front door bang shut.

Chapter 10

Sarah's gaze lingered on her mobile's glowing screen. Linda was calling for the third time today. Bringing the phone to her ear, Sarah answered.

"It's been a month, where have you been? And why are you avoiding my calls?" Linda's voice came through the phone.

A wry smile curled the corners of Sarah's lips. "Mark hasn't let me stay alone at night. Cinema, restaurants, museum visits," she whispered.

"Poor princess," Linda teased. "Do your diamond shoes hurt?"

"You know what I mean. But I haven't stopped practicing."

"How?"

"I am taking private classes with Diego almost daily during lunchtime. I've never looked thinner. But I haven't had the chance to dance at a milonga."

"Do you want me to come over?" Linda asked.

"To do what?"

"To practice."

"Practice?" Sarah repeated, confused.

"I know how to lead."

"Women do that?"

"Much better than most men," Linda said.

Sarah laughed. "When do you want to..." She paused as the doorbell rang. "Wait, someone's at the door." Peering through the peephole, she gasped. "Are you crazy? Mark's here!"

"Open it," Linda said and hung up the phone.

"Get inside."

Smiling, Linda entered and hung her jacket on the coat rack. She walked into the living room and immediately noticed the floor. "You know you have a perfect floor for tango, right?"

"Tango people give weird compliments," Sarah smiled. "And yes, I practice my pivots here."

"I know."

Sarah looked at Linda, confused. Linda pointed toward a circular mark on the floor.

"Did my heels do that?" Sarah kneeled and tried to erase the black line with her nail.

"Yep. And it means you keep your heels on the floor while pivoting. Good job."

Sarah listened to Mark's footsteps and lifted her index finger to her lips.

"I thought I heard someone's voice," Mark said. "Hi, I am Mark," he said, offering his hand for a handshake. Linda ignored it and went straight for a hug. Sarah smiled as she saw Mark's surprised face. "You snagged one of the good ones, Sarah," Linda said, winking at Mark.

Mark's face brightened and turned a tiny bit red. "Do you work together at the hospital?" he asked.

"I supply their shoes," Linda replied without missing a beat.

"I didn't know they had to wear special shoes. I'm learning new things every day," he said. "Well, I guess you've got to wear something comfortable if you're going to be in them for hours, don't you?"

"Comfort and stability, that's our signature," Linda bowed.

Mark laughed. "Comfort and stability could be my motto too," he said, looking at Sarah. "Pumpkin, I have to go out. Enjoy the company." He turned toward Linda, "I hope to see you again soon, and maybe that time I'll catch your name."

"Maybe," Linda smiled.

Mark grabbed his green jacket and smiled one last time before leaving.

"He is cute, well done," she said to Sarah, looking at the door's frosted glass. The green silhouette faded. "You should bring him to a class."

"What do I say when he asks me what's your name?"

"My middle name is Joana if that helps."

"Well, Joana, help me push this couch away, will you?"

They swiftly cleared the room.

"Let me connect my phone to your speakers," Linda said, tapping a few buttons.

Electronic beats merged with melodies, bandoneon and violins weaving through. But Sarah could also hear dub elements and modern beats. "Is this tango?"

"Better. It's Gotan," Linda smiled and invited her to the middle of the room.

There was something cinematic about this music, as if the dance floor became a scene in a movie.

"Let's see what you learned these weeks," Linda said.

Sarah took a few steps toward Linda and stopped.

Linda looked at her confused face. "I think you are wasting your money on those privates," Linda said playfully.

"It's just that... I don't know how to embrace you. You have..."

"I have what?" Linda smiled.

"Uhh... Boobs."

Linda looked down and then looked up again, feigning surprise. "That's what they are! I was breaking my head over these for years," she said. "So?"

Sarah shrugged. "Should I embrace you as I embrace Diego?"

"Sure, show me the magic."

"Oh dear, you are not ready for the magic yet," Sarah smiled.

Stepping closer, Sarah embraced Linda, and took a few steps together.

"What do you feel is different?" Linda asked.

"Your embrace is much softer than Diego's."

"Good job, girls," said Linda, looking down at her chest.

"Not that. Well, that too. But your hands are also softer. They move more."

"I use a more flexible embrace than Diego's. I believe it gives my partners more freedom to move. What else?" Linda led a few side steps in a row.

"I feel your center is different."

"My center of mass is lower than Diego's. It's because I am shorter, and because of those two bad boys," she said, shaking her hips left and right. "You are good at noticing, what else?"

"I don't know," Sarah said.

"Well, that was good enough," Linda said. "My turn. Your embrace is wonderful, I understand why guys love it. But your feet lack expression. They're holding back your dance. Look," Linda said, taking a step to the left. "Now, look again." She stepped to the right. "What do you see?"

"You're doing side steps, left and right."

"Now look closer." Linda executed a side step to the left slowly. She pointed at the orientation of her left foot as it landed, then at her right foot, still pushing the floor to propel her body. Finally, she gestured toward her right foot as she brought it close to the left, uniting the two. She mirrored the action to the other side, while Sarah's eyes followed every detail.

"I think I understand." Sarah stepped sideways, angling her left foot outward. She slowly brought her right foot beside the left, tilting it slightly so only the inside of the right foot touched the floor. She wobbled and steadied herself with her hand.

"Try it a few more times, as slow as you can. Focus on the wall, right above the clock. It will help with your posture."

Sarah glanced at the clock. 16:13. Her lips were slightly pursed, and a faint furrow marked her brow.

Linda corrected her multiple times, readjusting her feet. "No need to clench your fists," Linda advised. "Push the floor with your leg until the last moment, it helps create the lines you want. Good. Now, keep your hips level. You'll feel more stable if you tilt your head toward the free leg. "

"I feel like a robot," Sarah said. "It's hard to coordinate everything."

"Do you want a break?"

"No, I need to get this. Push, foot, tilt, collect. And don't clench my fists. Plus, keep smiling." Sarah repeated the steps.

Linda circled her, adjusting Sarah's hips and ankles, pulling her shoulders back. With each correction, Sarah inhaled deeply and tried again.

"Now, feel the music. Imagine a scene in your head and let it lead you," Linda suggested.

Sarah tuned into the music, reminiscent of a film soundtrack. Closing her eyes, she pictured a sultry, enigmatic woman descending the stairs of an abandoned building, clad in a tight leather jacket, black pants, and high heels. She stepped to the side once more.

Linda nodded. "This is it! Hold onto that image, use it when you need inspiration. Now, try this," Linda said. She executed a slow side step left, her right leg suddenly whipping across in front of her left, creating an elegant arc in the air before rejoining her other foot. "That's a *boleo*. Try it with me."

After a few attempts, Sarah said, "It looks silly when I do it."

"Focus on your hip, not your feet."

Sarah's next try was quicker, the boleo more fluid.

"See, the hips do more than just lower our center of gravity," Linda said with a smile. "Let's do it together. Embrace me."

Sarah tried a few more times. "I feel I am grabbing you for balance to do this. Wouldn't this bother the leaders?"

"You'll learn how to do it in a way that doesn't block his movement. You will also learn how to slow him down or show him that you want him to move faster."

"I thought it's their job to lead," Sarah said, taking a step back.

"How cute," Linda smiled. "Look, you have two choices. You can enter this tango world of ours and define yourself as a beginner. Or, you can define yourself as a woman and bring this energy to your dance," she said, lifting Sarah's chin with a finger. Sarah straightened up.

"Do you think a good leader wants a passive partner? Someone who doesn't add to the dance or just waits for him to lead?" Linda questioned.

"No?"

"Heck no. It's okay to be more careful in the beginning, focusing only on following. But the real pleasure comes when you learn to communicate your needs without saying a word, through this," she said, pointing to her embrace. "If you need more time for a movement, you can slow him down. And if he's a good dancer, he'll feel it. That's when your tango truly sparkles. But that's not the highest level. There's one more level beyond that," Linda said, her eyes gleaming mischievously and flashing a broad smile.

Sarah leaned in.

"When both partners are attuned to the music, you anticipate the rhythm and mood together, even if you don't know the exact steps." Linda demonstrated, moving quickly to the rhythm, then slowing with the melody. A violin's soft strains filled the room as Linda traced circles on the floor with her feet. When the bandoneon's beat returned, she executed rapid boleos. After turning down the music, Linda asked, "Did the timing of my steps make sense?"

Sarah nodded.

"Tango shows its true nature when you can both hug each other and let your common understanding of the music move you. Then, through the embrace, you will communicate your needs to each other. In one dance, you can feel understood, cared for, and connected..."

Sarah looked captivated, smiling.

"...Unless you define yourself by how many classes you've taken or how long you've danced," Linda finished, causing Sarah to laugh. "It's a journey. You work on yourself. You learn connection and communication, you learn how to understand the music. And finally, you just let go."

"Can you show me how to communicate through the embrace whether I want to move fast or slow?" Sarah asked.

"You don't get tired, do you?" Linda smiled.

"Not until I learn it all."

Linda looked at her for a few seconds, silent.

"What?" Sarah grinned.

"You can't learn it all in classes, Sarah. The real tango happens in the milongas." Linda let the words sink in.

Sarah's smile faded and she slumped onto the sofa. "How do I tell him?"

"As a woman," Linda advised.

Sarah glanced at the clock. "Crap!" She jumped up. "Quick, the sofa."

Linda watched, amused, as Sarah struggled to push the sofa in her high heels. "Pumpkin, you've never looked sexier."

Sarah paused. "I'll talk to him tonight, OK? But first, help me tidy up," she said.

"I don't think we have time," Linda pointed to the door.

Sarah paled as the frosted glass door tinted green and the sound of keys jingled in the hallway.

Mark entered. "You're still here," he said, smiling at Linda. He took off his jacket and walked into the living room. "So, what's your..." Then he noticed Linda's heels and paused. His eyes moved to Sarah's feet. "I see. Comfort and stability," he said as he realized what they were.

Linda grabbed her bag from the couch and walked toward the exit. "Listen to what she has to say. She needs this."

"This is none of your business... Linda," he said quietly.

"Good guess," Linda said. "Now, use this smart brain of yours to understand what she is trying to tell you." Linda glanced at Sarah one last time behind Mark's back. She put her thumb on her own chin and pushed it up.

Sarah listened to the door closing and looked at Mark. She could see his jaw muscles clenching.

"Why are you afraid of this?" she asked.

"And by 'this' you mean going out alone, hugging people I don't know, having drinks, and who knows what else?" Mark asked.

"By 'this' I mean dancing. If you tried it, you might feel differently about it. Why don't you take a class with me?"

Mark's expression softened. "You *want* me to come with you?"

"Together is always better," Sarah said, walking closer to him.

He hesitated. "Look, I'll do it for you. One class."

"Yes?" Sarah smiled.

"One class."

Sarah wrapped her hands around him. "Now that deserves a celebration."

"Are you planning to keep those heels on?" Mark asked.

"You tell me. The class starts in an hour."

58

Chapter 11

"Who is this young gentleman?" Maria asked, looking at Mark.

Sarah took him by the hand. "Maria, meet Mark. Is it okay if he joins us today?"

"We can always use more men," said Maria. "Welcome to the class, Mark. This way, please." She pointed toward the dance floor. "Enjoy!"

"Did you hear that?" Mark chuckled as they walked together to the middle of the dance floor. "Apparently, I am a *young* gentleman."

Sarah smiled at Maria, who gave her a knowing wink.

Jessica's voice cut through the chatter. "Everyone, thirty seconds to start! Guys on the right side, women on the left."

As Sarah's gaze shifted from Mark to Jessica, she observed her long black skirt cascading down to her ankles. As Jessica walked toward the front of the class, the skirt parted, revealing a bold slit that ascended along her right leg, reaching her upper thigh. Her top was as revealing as her skirt, leaving her belly and shoulders bare, and as she turned, the expanse of her back came into view.

"Diego?" Sarah mouthed toward Maria, who was standing on her left.

Maria shook her head from side to side. "No."

"Everybody, roll your shoulders back," Jessica instructed.

Sarah watched Jessica's back as she spoke. *Gosh, that woman has no fat on her,* she thought. She admired, with a tinge of jealousy, how Jessica's shoulder blades moved with sensual elegance, little muscles appearing and disappearing in mere moments. *I bet she chose that exercise to show off her back.*

"Sarah, will you join us?" Jessica asked.

Sarah realized that everyone else was standing behind Jessica, mimicking the movement. Mark leaned forward in the front row, his eyes intently fixed on Jessica, absorbing every move. Sarah quickly joined him.

"Everyone, do a lapice with your right leg," Jessica instructed. She then extended her right leg forward and drew a large circle with it. As the skirt opened, everyone could see her leg moving gracefully.

Sarah stared at it. It was toned, a perfect balance between muscle definition and feminine curvature. From the strong thigh that powered her intricate footwork to the sculpted calf that gracefully articulated each movement, every part of her leg was like visual poetry. *I remember when I had skin like that*, she thought. Sarah looked at the mirror, trying and failing to catch Mark's gaze. He was as mesmerized by Jessica as everyone else.

"Sarah, wake up. Big circles, your legs look dead," Jessica said.

Sarah paused for a few seconds. *Did she actually say that to me?* She lifted her chin, nodding firmly at Jessica and focused on replicating the movement.

"Everyone, continue," Jessica said and began correcting each student individually. When she reached Mark, she smiled. "When you do the circle, start the movement from your hips," she said softly and placed her hand on his hips. "Open your legs from the inside, from here." Her fingers guided Mark's inner thigh, drawing it subtly toward her. "Big circle. What's your name?"

A wave of irritation washed over Sarah. She turned away, her gaze finding her reflection in the mirror. She took a moment to recall Linda's advice from their earlier practice session. *Straight lines. Be a woman. What is she doing now? Focus. Who does she think she is?* Sarah's jaw clenched, her hands balling into fists at her sides. "Focus," she whispered under her breath, trying to steady her racing thoughts.

Jessica paused beside Sarah, scrutinizing her for a fleeting moment before moving on to the next student without a word. As Sarah processed the silent critique, Jessica's voice echoed through the room, "Everyone, find a partner!"

Sarah approached Mark with a smile.

"Sarah, please come here. He doesn't know how to walk yet. I need to show him," Jessica called from across the room. "Mark, come here. Everyone, embrace."

Sarah gave a polite smile to a short, middle-aged man with a prominent belly who stood before her. As he embraced her, she couldn't help but glance over his shoulder at Mark. Jessica moved her hand elegantly, placing it on Mark's neck and then sliding her fingers up to the back of his head. She leaned her forehead against Mark's, rotating her head within the embrace. Sarah could see their lips, almost close enough that a single breath could bridge the gap. And then she saw Jessica smiling.

"Everyone, walk," Jessica commanded. She then began speaking softly to Mark.

As Sarah's partner started dancing, she found herself unable to see Mark. Deciding to close her eyes, she focused on her walk, ensuring her legs appeared long and elegant with each step. Occasionally, she heard Mark's and Jessica's voices nearby, but she kept her eyes closed.

The class moved through various exercises, and with each new one, Sarah tried, yet failed, to pair up with Mark. Jessica didn't let him go.

"Everyone, who knows what a gancho is?" Jessica asked, and the room fell silent. "Mark, please extend your left leg forward," she said as she approached him. "Now, bend that knee slightly. Can everyone see the space under Mark's leg?" She positioned herself to his left, their hips touching. "What happens if I try to make a big circle with my right leg and meet his leg along the way?" She extended her leg forward, then moved it to the right. Her thigh brushed against Mark's, and she bent her knee, her leg wrapping around his. "That's a gancho," she announced. "Try it."

Sarah caught a fleeting look of discomfort in Mark's eyes, a flash of unease as he realized she was about to wrap her legs around another man's. "I'll try it with Mark," she declared, approaching him.

Jessica shot a quick, searching glance at Sarah before turning away to her laptop.

Sarah forced a smile and placed her arm around Mark's neck. A flicker of discomfort crossed Mark's face before he settled into an unreadable expression. She positioned herself to his left, attempting to mimic Jessica's movement. Mark's embrace was stiff and

61

reluctant. They stumbled through the new step, their movements out of sync, losing balance with each awkward attempt. Sarah sensed something was off but couldn't pinpoint what.

Jessica approached them, watching them fail with a small smile on her face. "Some people are not made for tango," she whispered, moving on to the next couple.

Sarah looked at Mark, shocked. His eyes were as cold and emotionless as his embrace. *That's it, we are getting out of here,* she thought.

"We are done for today," Jessica announced with a big smile. "See you next week." A gentle wave of applause washed over the room as she gave a graceful, practiced bow.

Sarah didn't wait a second longer and approached Maria. "Where is Diego?" she asked.

"He's at the marathon," she replied.

Sarah's brow furrowed in confusion. "He runs?"

Maria laughed softly. "No, not running. A tango marathon. It's a big event, three days of non-stop dancing. I am surprised he didn't mention it to you."

Maria noticed Mark approaching. "How was the class, young man?"

He offered a noncommittal shrug, "It was okay, I guess. Sarah, let's go?"

Sarah exchanged a brief, knowing look with Maria.

As they walked to the car, the transition from the vibrant energy of the dance studio to the cool night air felt abrupt. Mark's silence enveloped them.

Sarah, lost in her thoughts, barely noticed the familiar streets passing by as he drove. After a while, she pulled out her mobile, seeking Linda's contact. "Do you know anything about a tango marathon? Diego went there, he didn't say anything," she texted and placed her mobile, screen down, on her lap. She looked at Mark, his gaze fixed on the road ahead, the passing streetlights casting fleeting shadows across his focused expression. "Look, the classes are not usually like that. I think Jessica doesn't like me and just tried to make us feel jealous."

"Why do you think she doesn't like you?"

Sarah paused, weighing her words. "It's just a feeling," she said. "Did you enjoy it?" she asked, but she could hear the defeat in her own voice.

Mark sighed. "You know, if I were single, I might have actually loved this. Jessica is good. But I am not single. Neither are you. And you listened to what she said. Some people are just not made for tango, and according to her, I am not one of them."

"She was talking about me, Mark, not about you," Sarah said.

"Well, it seems I agree with her."

Sarah clenched her fists, a turmoil of emotions brewing silently within her. *Why was Jessica there, of all days, why today?* The mobile vibrated in her pocket. 'It's uptown. Below is the link to the event. Registrations are closed, but ask for James when you arrive. He is the organizer and a good friend of mine. He told me he'll let you in.'

Taking a deep, steadying breath, Sarah talked softly. "Look, I understand that you don't like tango. But I do. I didn't enjoy the class, I wanted to dance with you, and she didn't let us. And..." She took a long pause. "...And I am going to dance tonight. If you want, you can join me, so that you can see for yourself that there is nothing to worry about."

For the rest of the ride home, Mark remained silent. Upon arriving, he parked the car with mechanical precision and exited. Without looking back, he walked towards the house. He absentmindedly removed his shoes, his actions automatic, and trudged upstairs, lost in his own thoughts.

Sarah followed suit, her mind a whirlwind of emotions. She entered the bedroom and picked up a dress and her dance shoes, her movements slow, burdened by the heavy air.

Turning to leave, she paused, her gaze inadvertently drawn to Mark. He lay on the bed still fully clothed, his eyes unblinkingly fixed on the ceiling. She took a tentative step closer. Seconds stretched out, filled only by a quiet tension. But he remained still. With a resigned sigh, Sarah turned away.

Preferring not to drive at night, she called an Uber and waited outside, lost in thought. She looked a few times up at the window, but there was no light or movement. She pulled out her mobile. 'I am coming,' she typed. A black Ford Focus stopped in front of her. As she stepped into the car, she cast one last, lingering look upward, a silent wish for understanding. For a brief moment, she thought she saw the curtains stir. She turned on the passenger's light and pulled out her makeup pouch.

"Would you like me to wait for a few minutes?" the driver asked.

"Yes, please."

"Getting ready for a night out?"

"I am going to a marathon," she said.

The driver took a long look at her through the mirror. "If you say so," he smiled. "Just let me know when you are ready," he said.

Chapter 12

"James, this is my friend Sarah," Linda said. He was athletic, in his early forties, dressed in black tango trousers and a crisp, white, long-sleeved shirt. James pulled her gently into a warm embrace.

"Linda told me to keep an eye on you," James said with a wink as he stepped back. "She said you're going to break many hearts soon. Was it easy to find this place?"

"Yes," Sarah replied, glancing quickly at Linda. "Thank you so much for accepting me at such short notice."

"A friend of Linda's is a friend of mine," James said, placing a thin bracelet around her wrist. "This is for you to enter the main venue," he explained, pointing to a door on their right. "Also, please don't tell anyone you decided to join today. We have a waiting list of over a hundred followers. They would be up in arms."

Sarah drew her finger across her lips, mimicking a zipper, and then tossed the imaginary key over her shoulder.

"Now, Linda mentioned this is your first marathon. I'm honored to be your first host. Do you have any questions I can answer?"

Where is Diego? Sarah thought. She smiled. "For starters, what exactly is a marathon?"

James laughed, his eyes twinkling with passion. "It's where tango dreams come true," he said, his voice reminiscent of a magician telling a story. "Guys, I'll be inside for a while. We have an important guest here." He then turned to Sarah and offered his elbow. Sarah looked at Linda, who nodded encouragingly. She looped her arm through his, feeling like a million bucks.

"What a gentleman," she remarked.

"Every lady deserves a gentleman," he replied smoothly, and they walked into the main venue.

Sarah's mouth dropped open. "Wow, this place is huge," she exclaimed. Oversized white balloons hung from the ceiling, hovering above the dance floor. Their hues ranged from bold, passionate reds to deep purples. The warm glow of festival lights reflected off their surfaces, casting a kaleidoscope of colors throughout the venue.

65

Below this vibrant display, hundreds of tango dancers moved gracefully, their silhouettes illuminated by the balloons' glow. As she took in the scene, Sarah began searching the crowd. *Where is Diego?*

Chairs and tables surrounded the dance floor. The chairs were elegant and cushioned, and the tables were covered with pristine white tablecloths. Drinks, light refreshments, and a selection of snacks and dried fruits were available. Groups of people gathered around the tables, their laughter and animated conversations creating a delightful hum. Every so often, a man would approach a table, and a smiling woman would stand up, ready to dance. *Where is he?*

"Come with me, this way," James guided Sarah through the crowd with care.

At the far end of the venue, Sarah noticed the DJ's stand, elevated slightly for visibility. It hosted a sleek console. The DJ, a tall man in his fifties, had a collection of vinyl records behind him, neatly organized. A projected image revealed his name as Gaston. He took out a record and placed its case in front of the console for everyone to see. The cover displayed a man in dark glasses.

"I know this music," Sarah exclaimed with the enthusiasm of a seven-year-old receiving a birthday gift.

"Bahia Blanca, a wonderful piece. This recording is by the orchestra of Di Sarli."

"Is that the guy on the cover with the dark glasses?" *And where is Diego?*

"Yes. He always wore those, even in dark venues."

Sarah's eyebrows shot up in exaggerated surprise. "Why would he do that?"

"He hardly ever took them off in public. Many people misinterpreted it as arrogance. The truth is, when he was a teenager, a gun shop assistant accidentally shot him while cleaning a gun. Di Sarli began wearing dark glasses to hide his injured eye. That's why one of his nicknames was El Tuerto, the One-Eyed. Once, while playing with his orchestra, a club owner told him to stop being silly and take off his glasses. Di Sarli didn't like it and left. The whole orchestra followed him."

66

"They just left?"

"That's what they say. Perhaps one day we can share a *mate*, and I'll tell you more stories. For now, here's what you need to know. You can sit anywhere you like. We are one big family. If you want to sit with Linda, her table is the one with the pink candle. Drinks at the bar are free, and the milonga lasts until 5, so pace yourself. Please never walk across the dance floor, always go around it. If anything makes you feel uncomfortable, come and find me immediately. And," he paused, holding her hand in his, "enjoy." He gave her a hug and walked away toward the entrance.

Sarah approached Linda's table, sat down, and placed her belongings on an empty chair. She noticed Linda's shoe bag on the chair, emblazoned with vibrant gold letters reading "Tango Shoes for Life." It was positioned so everyone on the dance floor could easily see it. *She is good*, Sarah thought, smiling. She proudly pulled her heels from the bag, admiring them for a few seconds. *Do people hug their heels often enough?*

She bent down, her fingers lightly grazing her heels' slender straps. Effortlessly, she slid her feet into their alluring embrace. *Those legs look sexy*, she mused and a cascade of confidence enveloped her. Then, she saw him.

His white shoes caught her eye first, dancing elegantly on the polished floor. His legs moved confidently, each step a testament to his mastery of tango. She observed his calm, peaceful face, a kind smile playing on his lips. Her gaze then shifted to his dance partner, whose face radiated pure bliss. *Of course, she's dancing with Diego.*

She waved at him, but he didn't seem to notice. Feeling foolish, Sarah lowered her hand. She pulled her phone from her purse and opened the Messages app, only to find no new messages. "Should I be relieved or worried?" she whispered to herself. She slowly typed, "I miss you here," her finger hovering over the Send button. After a few seconds, she deleted the message and put the phone back in her bag.

A cortina started playing, reminding her of a flamenco show she'd attended in Spain a few years ago. *Maybe Mark would be happier if I danced flamenco instead*, she thought.

"What are you doing here?" Diego asked, smiling.

Sarah stood up. "I'm trying to understand why you thought it was a good idea to not tell me about this," she said, her face cold and emotionless.

Diego stepped back, his smile fading. "I... No... I just thought that..."

Sarah burst into laughter. "I owed you one. Now, tell me why."

Diego sighed in relief. "I thought it might be too early for you to join. You've learned a lot, but most people at marathons have been dancing for at least ten years."

It was time for Sarah's smile to fade. "Linda didn't mention this," she said. "Can I... Can I just watch from a corner?"

Before Diego could respond, another figure emerged from the crowd, approaching with a relaxed stride. He appeared to be in his late sixties, his posture and eyes hinting at a handsome youth.

"Jonathan, this is Sarah. She started classes with me a few weeks ago."

Jonathan waved at Sarah. "Don't worry, you'll find better teachers soon. Don't quit yet," he said playfully.

His voice reminded Sarah of her father. "I had a feeling I was making the wrong choice with this one," she replied with a smile. "Are you his student too?"

Jonathan smiled. "This kiddo couldn't even spell 'tango' when I started dancing."

Sarah looked at Diego. "Didn't you say you started dancing when you were six?"

Diego nodded.

She turned to Jonathan. "Have you been dancing tango for thirty years?"

"Tango isn't counted in years, my dear. Listen, this is a wonderful tanda. Would you like to dance?"

Sarah's expression shifted from surprise to terror. "Oh no, I'm a beginner. I don't want to make your life hard," she said.

"If I can't lead a beginner, then I'm not much of a dancer, am I?" he replied, standing up.

Sarah glanced at Diego, pleading for help.

His smile stretched ear to ear. "Enjoy, I'll just sit here watching. Oh, wait!" He pulled out his phone. "You're going to want to remember this."

"No!" Sarah mouthed to Diego as Jonathan took her hand and led her toward the dance floor.

He stopped just before entering, looking at the couple behind them. The other leader nodded, and Jonathan stepped forward, offering his embrace.

Sarah's heart raced, her legs shaking slightly as her arm went around his shoulder. Jonathan seemed unhurried. He repositioned his hand on her back, moving his embrace slowly left and right, as if comforting a baby. He led a side step. Sarah stepped and immediately felt off balance, her legs still trembling. Jonathan appeared not to notice. He took a couple of steps, and turned left. Sarah now faced the chairs, where Diego was recording her with a huge, annoying smile. *What's with tango people recording without permission?*

Jonathan's steps were few and slow. It was as if he was letting most notes pass unnoticed. He simply chose one or two of them every now and then. His dance unfolded as a series of pauses, interrupted by a few perfectly timed steps.

Sarah noticed the pauses were not static. His embrace gently rocked, swaying left and right. She closed her eyes, and a distant memory unfurled. She was a little girl, waiting on the porch for her father's return from work. She always waited for him on the rocking chair. He would walk up the stairs, place his bag on the last step, and look at her. "How are you doing, princess?" he would ask. "I am better now," she would always respond. It was their little dialogue, practiced again and again, making them smile every single time. She would make space for him to sit, and she would lie on top of him, closing her eyes. They would gently rock back and forth. A couple of minutes later, he would ask about her day, listening intently as she shared everything important to her.

Sarah remembered the last day she waited on the porch. She had stayed for hours, ignoring her mother's pleas to come inside. Then the phone rang. Her mother came out minutes later, crying. She placed her hand on Sarah's diaphragm, a gesture she always made when she wanted to calm Sarah. "Come, honey, we need to visit your grandma. You'll sleep there tonight."

"Are you alright?" Jonathan asked gently, snapping her back to reality.

The song had ended, but Sarah didn't release the embrace. She felt her tears going down her cheek. She was still shaking, but differently now.

"I am sorry," she said, still hugging him.

"Don't be. Would you like to continue dancing?"

Sarah adjusted her embrace and said nothing. She kept her eyes closed for the next three songs. She allowed herself to remember everything. Step by step, the rocking embrace grew warmer, more intimate, more familiar.

Lost in the dance and her memories, Sarah barely noticed the music's end. Jonathan's gentle voice brought her back, his tone tender. As they parted, her heart was full, her eyes brimming with unshed tears. "Thank you," she whispered, her voice thick with emotion.

"Thank *you*," Jonathan echoed, his eyes reflecting similar depth. "I haven't felt so much tango in years."

Sarah wiped her tears, a smile touching her lips. "You said tango isn't measured in years. How do you measure it?"

Jonathan pulled a white pocket square from his suit and delicately wiped away her remaining tears. Folding it neatly, he returned it to its place and then guided her hand to rest on his heart.

"Heartbeats, honey, heartbeats."

Chapter 13

Jonathan offered Sarah his arm and walked her back to the table. "I'll leave you with your friends now. My fourth trip to the bathroom tonight is due. Five more and I'll call it a night," he said, smiling.

Sarah felt as though she was stepping from one world into another. She saw Linda and Diego deep in conversation and quietly slipped into a chair, her mind still echoing with the dance's emotional resonance.

"You don't get it, Diego," Linda said, interrupting Sarah's thoughts. "Experimenting with different music *is* what evolves my tango."

"What's going on?" Sarah asked.

"Your narrow-minded teacher here thinks he is the protector of all that is good and right in tango," Linda said.

Diego smiled. "Don't worry, I've known Linda for, what, eight years now?"

"Eight long years," Linda corrected him.

"What if we let Sarah decide?" Diego suggested. "Go ahead, make your point."

Linda turned to Sarah. "Think about our practice session today. Did the music we used help you dance better?"

Sarah hesitated, aware of Diego's gaze. "Yes, it did."

"And was it traditional tango music?" Linda pressed.

"Not really."

"There you go, case closed," Linda declared triumphantly.

Diego smiled. "Can I make my point now, or is it pointless? "

"You can. And it *is* pointless. "

Diego leaned in, his eyes twinkling. Sarah felt it took a bit longer than necessary, but she stared back at him, noticing once again his long, expressive lashes.

"Sarah, consider this. What's easier for a child to dance to? Beethoven's Fifth Symphony or something simple and catchy, like..." he began, singing, "the wheels on the bus go round and round, round and round, round and round?"

A few nearby dancers glanced over, and Linda burst into laughter. "Really, that's your argument? "

Sarah chuckled. "I would have to go with the wheels on the bus," she said.

"Exactly," Diego said. "It takes time and experience to appreciate the subtleties in music. But once you do, after all this dedication, the resonance and pleasure are so much deeper than any bus ride can offer."

Linda laughed. "You've clearly never ridden the right bus, Diego."

"And you have?" Sarah asked.

"More times than I care to admit," Linda said, and they all burst into laughter.

Their laughter was cut short as a young man in jeans and a T-shirt approached. His direct gaze landed on Sarah. "Do you want to dance?" he asked, extending his hand.

Sarah glanced at her friends, noticing Linda's and Diego's amused expressions. "Sure, let's go," she replied, rising from her chair.

As they stepped onto the dance floor the man placed a firm hand on her back. Without warning, he pulled her to the side, causing her to momentarily lose her balance. *Focus, Sarah*, she thought. As he initiated a rotation, she concentrated on following his lead, striving to sync with his movements. But his hand on her back completely blocked her. She felt a subtle pain in her lower back as she tried to pivot. Step after step, she felt lost, making all kinds of mistakes. When the first song finished, Sarah tried to take a step back, but his hand on her back didn't let her, keeping her there for a few more seconds.

"How long have you been dancing?" he asked, finally relaxing the embrace.

"About a month," Sarah said. She noticed him lifting one side of his mouth in a subtle smile.

"That's why. I have been dancing for almost two years now," he said proudly. "You know, you need to give me more resistance with your hands. Try pushing me a bit more. Also, your embrace is too relaxed, make it firm."

Sarah pushed her right hand a bit more and contracted a few muscles in her arms. It was easier to understand what he wanted now, but she still felt like a robot being carried around. As the music got faster, he led a few very big steps. Sarah felt her heel hitting someone behind her. She immediately released the embrace and turned her head back. An older lady was looking at her in pain.

"I am terribly sorry, I didn't see you," Sarah said.

"You are not dancing alone in this room, you know. You have to respect the others," her partner said and led the lady off the dance floor.

Sarah didn't know how to respond.

"Those old people don't know how to move on the dance floor," the man whispered to her. "Come on, let's continue."

Sarah embraced him again, but this time she kept her eyes open and her steps small. He stepped on her a few times because of this, but she would rather suffer herself than hit another person.

When the third song started, she noticed Diego and Linda entering the dance floor right in front of her. Jonathan and another lady positioned themselves behind her. *What's happening?* she thought as the song began. Diego started dancing, moving away from Sarah. Jonathan, on the other hand, seemed to be dancing on the spot. Sarah smiled. *They are creating space*, she realized. She winked at Linda, who was smiling at her.

As the final notes of the fourth song faded, the young man nodded and retreated into the crowd. Sarah stood momentarily disoriented, the echoes of the dance lingering uncomfortably.

Linda and Diego appeared at her side, each draping an arm around her shoulders. It felt like a protective cocoon against the jarring experience she'd just had. Together, they navigated through the dancers and made their way back to their table.

"That's one bus ride I never want to take again," Sarah said. "I have so much to learn."

Linda looked at Diego.

"You know, you don't need to go all the way to the terminal. That's what bus stops are for," Diego said.

"What do you mean?" Sarah asked.

"If the bus sucks, get off the bus, pumpkin. Another one will come," Linda said, grabbing her glass of wine from the table.

Sarah looked puzzled. "Can we stop with the bus metaphor, please?"

Linda looked at Diego. "In all your classes, you didn't think once to tell her that she doesn't have to dance the whole tanda with someone?"

Diego's eyes widened slightly and his eyebrows knit together in a small frown. His lips quirked to one side, and with a subtle tilt of his head, he gave the most innocent and endearing look he could muster. "Linda is right. You don't need to dance all four songs with someone. If you feel uncomfortable or in pain, you can stop after the first song," he said.

"You can stop after the first second if you choose to," Linda said. "Frankly, if a man comes to ask me without using the cabeceo, as your guy did, I usually say no. It's the gentlest way to ask, and it shows they respect me. Now," she looked toward Diego, "you owe me a proper dance, not one where I feel like a shield. Get your butt on the dance floor, I love this *vals*."

"I never felt more respected," Diego smiled and stood up. "The wheels on the bus go round and round, round and round," he sang while walking around Sarah's chair. Linda embraced him, put her right hand around his neck, and smacked his head from behind. Diego led an overly dramatic projection of the leg to the side and, laughing, they started swirling.

Sarah recognized the rhythm. Her mother loved listening to waltzes and dancing with her father at home. She remembered feeling jealous of them and trying to stop them. Her father would then lift her onto his shoulders. As young Sarah tapped the rhythm on his head, the three of them would dance together. Tango vals music was a bit different, but the sensation was the same. It was like flying on a cloud.

Her thoughts were interrupted when she noticed Jonathan coming back to the table, chatting animatedly with a woman. The same woman she had accidentally stepped on a while ago. Sarah's heart

74

skipped a beat, embarrassment coloring her cheeks. Jonathan, sensing her discomfort, offered a reassuring nod.

The old lady saw her and smiled. "Don't worry, sweetheart, you don't have eyes on your back. It's the man's responsibility to pay attention on the dance floor," she said. "And that young man doesn't know what he is doing."

Sarah put her hand on hers. "Still, I am terribly sorry. How is your foot?"

"This old thing? No worries, I don't feel most of it either way," she smiled. "How was your dance?"

"The first song was terrible. But then he asked me how long I had been dancing and gave me some corrections."

The old lady looked at Jonathan. "When will those young women learn not to listen to every random guy's opinion?" She turned to Sarah. "Darling, never trust someone just because they have been dancing longer than you. Actually, don't even ask them how long they have been dancing." She took a sip of her wine and paused. "I take it back. There is only one reason to truly ask a man how long he has been dancing." She leaned closer to Sarah with a playful expression. "To find out if the problem is permanent or if there is still hope." They laughed. "Now, let me tell you which ones you want to dance with before the night is over, and who will break your back if you let them."

"Alright, that's my cue," said Jonathan. "I'll let you gossip; I'll be back in a while." He stood up and held up five fingers to Sarah with a goofy smile.

Jackie pointed toward a few guys and explained why they would be a good match for Sarah. But Sarah's mind was elsewhere. She watched Diego and Linda glide across the floor, rotating with grace and smiling. She couldn't spot a single mistake in their dance. Diego would lead Linda, orchestrating her movements around him, and moments later, he would revolve around her. It was akin to two protagonists in a movie, allowing space for each other to shine and mutually building up their presence. But they were not the only ones.

Most of the dancers on the dance floor appeared to synchronize their movements, alternating between acceleration and deceleration simultaneously. Sarah noticed that each couple executed distinct steps, yet there was a quality that harmonized their motions. Sarah sensed an underlying nuance that transcended mere coordination but couldn't put her finger on it.

The tanda ended, and Diego came to the table.

"You look so nice together," Sarah said.

"We know how to adapt to each other," responded Linda. "The more you dance, the more you understand what your partners enjoy. Then you can give them more of what they like."

The cortina ended and the notes of a romantic violin filled the room. The lights dimmed to a soft red. Diego looked at Sarah and they stood up.

Sarah found that familiar spot right behind Diego's ear and placed her hand there. She felt Diego creating space in his chest. Closing her eyes, she melted into it, feeling his heartbeat and certain he could feel hers too. She matched her breathing with the rise and fall of his chest. Diego's hand gently caressed her back, tightening their embrace.

They began with a few slow steps. The deep voice of a singer enveloped the room, and Diego paused. Sarah could hear the sound of hundreds of feet moving on the floor around her. Lifting her hand slightly from his neck, barely touching him, she felt a delicate ripple through his skin, causing tiny, elevated bumps. Her heart began to race. The music grew more dramatic, intensifying as more instruments joined in. Diego inhaled deeply, his muscles tensing in preparation to accelerate. Mirroring his tension, she inhaled, ready for the crescendo. Suddenly, the music went silent. The sound of steps and chatter around them vanished, leaving an eerie quiet.

Two seconds later, the room erupted in sound. All the instruments burst into life, the rhythm of steps indicating everyone was moving. Sarah opened her eyes as Diego opened a bit the embrace, allowing her to extend her movement. She circled around him, each step picking up speed. She noticed almost everyone else was also moving in circles. Then, after half a minute, the music halted with two dramatic notes, bringing everyone to a stop in silence.

The room burst into applause, eyes turned toward the DJ. He held up a blue and yellow case of a vinyl disc and pointed at it. On it was a well-dressed gentleman wearing glasses, more reminiscent of a scientist than a musician.

"Pugliese," Diego said.

As the next song began, the clapping continued a moment longer before everyone returned to their partner.

Song after song, Sarah relished the long pauses and sudden accelerations, the tight embrace, and the moments it opened, giving her more space to move. *Pugliese*, she repeated in her head a few times, ensuring the name would stay with her.

As the music faded into a brief silence, marking the end of the set, Sarah felt a wave of exhilaration mixed with exhaustion wash over her. She carried the rhythm of the dance in her every step as she made her way to the table, her smile wide and eyes sparkling.

"I need water," she said to Linda, her voice a mix of satisfaction and thirst. Linda returned her smile with a knowing look. Sarah dropped into her chair, a pleasant fatigue settling in her limbs. She placed her bag on her lap, her hand absentmindedly skimming over papers, keys, and unrecognizable objects amidst the orchestrated chaos inside. Her fingers brushed against her mobile phone, which she pulled out and laid on the table, screen facing down. Picking up her water bottle, she took a satisfying sip, the cool liquid a sharp contrast to the warm air around her. Closing her eyes briefly, she took a deep breath, allowing the memories of the dance to linger a moment longer before returning to the present.

Turning her mobile over with her right hand, she clicked. Six missed calls and a message. Her eyes widened, and a furrow formed on her forehead. Her lips, once relaxed, tightened.

"Are you OK?" Linda asked, looking at her worriedly. The light from the mobile had caught her attention.

Sarah showed her the notifications.

"You've received a gift, Sarah. Don't let it go to waste for anyone. Do you realize how many people go through their entire lives without ever discovering something that makes them feel as you do?"

"He's a great guy," Sarah said. "Do you have any idea how hard it is to find a good one at my age, let alone one that I would trust to have children with? And... he loves me."

"If he does, he'll understand," Linda said, holding her hand. "I've seen hundreds of women go into tango, Sarah. No one had as much tango inside them as you. It makes you happy. Do you want me to read you the message?"

Sarah took a deep breath.

"There's no point. He must be sleeping at this hour." She put her mobile back in her pocket and looked around. A man's gaze met hers. He tilted his head to the side, and Sarah smiled.

Chapter 14

Sarah locked her car and took a moment to appreciate the tranquility of the morning. The scent of freshly baked bread wafted through the air as the first batches were pulled from the oven of her local bakery. The melodic chorus of birds waking up contrasted with the stillness of the streets. The trees on her street stood as dark silhouettes against the brightening sky, a peaceful scene that she savored before turning to ascend the stairs toward her front door.

The morning humidity left a delicate sheen on the sleek, modern steps. She held the key in her hand for a few extra seconds, staring at its smooth, matte finish with a slight curvature that rested comfortably in her hand.

As she inserted the key into the lock, the door suddenly swung open. Startled, she found Mark standing in the doorway, his appearance disheveled from a sleepless night. His eyes held a muted glaze, lacking their usual sparkle, and deep shadows pooled beneath them. Lines, usually subtle, now etched a temporary residency on his forehead and around his eyes. He was still wearing the same clothes as the night before.

The sight of him awake and waiting sent a swirl of emotions through her – surprise, guilt, and a faint trace of dread. *He's been awake all night... worrying? Or angry?* Sarah thought, a knot forming in her stomach. "I thought you were sleeping," she said.

"I guess everything is just fine then," he said. Mark's words were laced with biting sarcasm, his voice a blend of resignation and bitterness. As he turned to walk back inside, there was a heaviness in his steps.

Sarah hung her coat and left her bag on the floor underneath it. The kitchen was awash in the warm light of the morning sun, filtering through the sheer curtains. The familiar, comforting scent of coffee filled the room, mingling with the faint aroma of the freshly baked bread she'd passed by earlier.

"Scrambled eggs and orange juice are at the table. Would you like a crepe?" he said, holding the resealable bag with the mix inside.

Sarah took a few steps closer.

"I am sorry I didn't respond. I really thought you would be sleeping by the time I saw it."

Mark didn't respond.

"Thank you for this beautiful breakfast."

"Would you expect anything less from a five-star *hotel*?" Mark said, a hint of anger in his voice.

Sarah looked into his eyes. "Look, I'll tell you everything that happened during the night. I promise. But can you please tell me what you think."

"Why, will it make any difference?" Mark's irritation was apparent in his voice. "You'll do what you please either way, not giving a damn about our relationship."

Sarah felt a tightness in her chest. She closed her eyes for a brief second, memories flooding in—lazy Sundays in bed, laughter echoing in their first, modest apartment, dreams they spun together like delicate webs. Where had that easiness vanished? Opening her eyes, she met Mark's gaze, now so unfamiliar.

"And that comes from the man who doesn't have time for a trip with me, who doesn't even talk about children anymore, who hasn't even thought to propose, leaving me uncertain about where we're heading?"

Mark's voice trembled. "Do you remember when we were both struggling, how we'd spend nights dreaming of a better future? I worked, and I am still working hard to create that future for us." In a sudden burst of anger, Mark hurled the crepe's container towards the sink. His jaw was set, and his hands clenched briefly into fists at his sides after the throw. "You are OK with this amazing house," Mark said, starting to count with his fingers, "OK with enjoying any restaurant we want, OK with drinking wine that none of your friends can afford, but you are not OK with me doing what I must do to provide this life?"

"I was a thousand times happier when we had nothing, when we just had time for each other and explored life together," Sarah said.

"So, you were lying to me all these years?" Mark said. "Here I am, busting my butt at work, to make sure that you have a wonderful life, and then at the first opportunity, you tap dance out of it."

Sarah burst. "Are you saying that I have contributed nothing to this magnificent life of yours? Do you even realize how many times..."

Mark walked out of the kitchen and up the stairs to the bedroom.

Sarah's eyes narrowed with intensity, and her knuckles turned pale. "I didn't finish talking, come back here," Sarah shouted. No response. She ran up the stairs, forcefully striking each step with all her strength, and swung the bedroom door open. Mark walked out carrying a pair of pants, a shirt, and his car keys.

"I have to go to work. This is your last warning. Make a choice," he said, running down the stairs.

The silence of the house enveloped Sarah as she stood motionless, absorbing the weight of their words. Sunlight streamed through the window, casting long shadows across the floor and highlighting the dust particles dancing in the air. She heard the front door banging. She collapsed to her knees, her hands covering her face as a raw wail escaped her lips. Frustration, sadness, and a sense of helplessness overwhelmed her, each emotion vying for dominance. Tears went down her cheeks and fell on the soft red Persian carpet below her, Mark's gift for her last birthday. Drop by drop, the wool absorbed them.

"Why?" Sarah said between her teeth. "Why don't you understand?" She looked down and noticed the red color had become darker. She looked at her fingers, black with washed-out eyeliner. "Crap. Mark will kill me," she said and ran to the bathroom. She came back with toilet paper in her hand. She placed it on the stain and rubbed it a bit. When she removed the paper, the stain looked worse. Instead of a few black drops here and there, she was now looking at a dark red mush. She tried one more time, but the result was the same.

She tossed the paper aside, feeling overwhelmed, and sat on her butt. She picked up her phone and dialed Linda, seeking the comfort of a familiar voice.

"What are you doing awake?" Linda asked.

"Do you have a couch?"

Linda stayed silent for a few seconds. "Come."

Sarah's gaze eventually fell to the black stains as she placed the mobile on the red carpet, prompting a shift in her focus. A thought struck her, and she moved towards her wardrobe, her movements now deliberate. She grabbed her red tango shoes and a black dress and placed them on the carpet, around the stain. "That seems about right," she whispered. She pulled her mobile from her pocket and took a few photos. Then, she packed.

Chapter 15

As the taxi driver turned into Linda's street, Sarah had no doubt which house was hers. The exterior, painted in vibrant hues of blues and greens, immediately set it apart from its neighbors.

Sarah walked through the front garden, a canvas of blossoming flowers and potted plants. She noticed a small bench, painted in whimsical patterns on the right side.

Linda's face, etched with worry, appeared at the window, her eyes widening as she caught sight of Sarah. In an instant, she disappeared from the window, reappearing seconds later at the door. Rushing out, her hands trembled slightly as she reached out, gently cupping Sarah's cheeks. "Oh, honey, you're here," Linda exclaimed, her voice a blend of relief and worry. "Come in, I've made some tea." She took Sarah's luggage from her, pointing towards the entrance with a welcoming gesture.

As Sarah stepped inside, the fragrances of blooming flowers mingled with the subtle aroma of fresh paint.

"I hope you don't mind the smell of fresh paint. I know it can be a bit overwhelming for some," Linda remarked, observing Sarah's reaction with a slightly apologetic smile.

"I like it," Sarah responded. "Do you paint?"

Linda stepped into the living room and waved to Sarah to come in. A half-finished portrait of two tango dancers in mid-motion was next to the window. The silhouettes emerged boldly in detail. Sarah could see the subtle arch of an eyebrow, the hint of a smile, and the delicate play of light on their entwined bodies. The lower half of the painting remained a dance of brushstrokes.

"It's only half-finished," Linda admitted, a note of artistic criticism in her tone as she glanced at the portrait. "I still need to decide what their legs will be doing. Sit down, I'll bring you tea, and you'll tell me what happened."

Sarah sat on the couch. It was full of pillows, each one adorned with various textures, from soft velvets to embroidered fabrics. A handmade throw blanket with a tango couple on it draped elegantly over one side of the couch. Sarah placed her mobile on one of the small, mismatched side tables that surrounded the couch. Art books, vintage vases, and small sculptures were all around. On the left, a grand piano was adorned with sheet music and framed photographs of tango events.

"Do you play?" Sarah asked when Linda entered the room.

"My father taught me," Linda's expression softened. "He was quite the musician," she reminisced, handing Sarah a cup of tea. "And this is from my last trip to China. Isn't it adorable?"

Sarah looked at the cup. The light played on the smooth surface, revealing the subtle translucency of the porcelain. "They look wonderful. You have a wonderful house."

Linda looked around. "I love to buy things from every place I travel. Most of those I bought in little local markets. Now," she said and turned her whole body toward Sarah, "what happened?"

"Mark... he was awake, waiting for me. We... we ended up fighting," she said, her voice quivering. "He cornered me into making a choice, Linda. I felt so trapped, so suffocated... and now, here I am."

Linda remained silent.

"Maybe this will help," Sarah said. She put the cup on the table, pulled her mobile from her bag, and clicked on the last photo.

Linda took the mobile from Sarah's hands and carefully zoomed in on the photo, her fingers gently pinching the screen as she studied the image.

"Eyeliner," said Sarah, starting to cry.

"Oh dear," Linda said, holding Sarah in a tender embrace. "Look, you needed some space, and you came here. You did the right thing. Sometimes, stepping away is the bravest choice." Linda paused, giving Sarah a moment. "And you have nothing to worry about, you can stay here for as long as you need."

The sound of the word 'long' hit Sarah hard. She felt her body shaking again. Linda stayed silent, hugging her for a few minutes.

As the shaking got weaker, Linda opened the embrace and looked at Sarah. "You just need to promise me one thing," she said with a serious frown above her eyes. She used her index finger to wipe some of Sarah's tears.

"What?" Sarah asked.

With a deeply worried face, Linda put her arms on Sarah's shoulders. "That you will never, ever, ever cry above my carpets."

Sarah's eyes widened for a split second, and then they both burst into laughter.

"Thank you," Sarah said after a while.

Linda smiled. "You must be exhausted after everything. Your room's ready, just down the hall, the one with the yellow door. Let's both try to get some rest, alright? Life is always better after a good sleep, a good dance, and a good song."

"Will you sing to me?" Sarah asked.

"Get that beautiful butt off my couch," Linda teased with a playful grin.

Sarah went up a ramp and walked down the hallway. An unusually large door led to her room. She left her luggage next to the bed. It had a few levers on the side. Sarah's fingers traced over the levers, a faint smile touching her lips. "Comfort and stability," she mused softly, a longing in her voice. As the back of the bed rose with a smooth motion, she couldn't help but imagine sinking into the plump pillows, finding solace from her chaotic thoughts. A plush armchair with a soft throw blanket draped over it was placed next to the window. Sarah drifted closer, her gaze settling on the lush greenery of Linda's backyard. It looked like a hidden oasis, a peaceful refuge that stood in stark contrast to the storm raging inside her. Next to the armchair, a small bookshelf held a collection of literature. Sarah's eyes wandered to the bookshelf. She tilted her head to read the titles. *Tangofulness, tango tips by the maestros, how to dance more in milongas*. "Later," Sarah whispered.

She moved her luggage close to the small open wardrobe. She noticed a blue blanket with a red race car on it and a few pillow covers with the same design at the bottom. The gentle aroma of lavender emanated from a carefully hung bouquet of dried lavender. As she began to unpack, her fingers brushed across the fabrics, each item sparking a different thought, memories of simpler times. She arranged her clothes, her movements slow, her mind wandering.

She reached for the curtains, pulling them closed. A beam of light could still pass from the side, but that didn't bother her. She wore her cat-themed pajamas and crawled into bed, staring at the dust particles dancing into existence and then oblivion.

Chapter 16

It wasn't until she heard Linda singing that she realized there was no more sun coming into the room. As her senses adjusted, she slowly rotated in the cocoon of her bed and looked for her mobile. 8:52pm. Her eyes focused on the screen – one missed call, one message reading, 'Where are you?' For a moment, Sarah just stared at the words, her mind eerily calm amidst the storm of recent events.

Then, her fingers moved fast. 'Sorry, I just woke up. I needed some space, so I went to Linda's place. I am going to sleep here tonight. We are not what we used to be, and before I put us through more fights, I need to understand my own thoughts and feelings. I love you, I am still yours, but I need to understand this. I am sorry. I am not ready to talk. I hope you can understand.'

She left the mobile next to her and stayed tucked for a few more minutes, looking at the ceiling. She heard Linda walk around the house, singing to the tune of a tango song playing on the sound system. After a while, she smelled fried bacon. "That's my cue," Linda said with a soft smile, rising from her bed and gracefully making her way out of the room.

"Hello, catwoman," Linda said.

Sarah looked down at her pajamas, did an exaggerated stretch, and licked the back of her right hand. "Catwoman smelled bacon," she said.

Linda put a slice on a plate and gave it to her.

Sarah took a moment to enjoy the smell and took a bite.

"Better than Diego's embrace?" Linda asked.

Sarah nodded. "They both make me warm inside," she smiled.

"And the best part? Unlike Diego's classes, this one is cruelty-free," Linda said with a playful wink.

Sarah paused mid-bite, her surprise evident. "This isn't bacon?" she asked, her eyebrows arching inquisitively.

"It tastes like bacon, feels like bacon, makes you happy like bacon, but the three little pigs are still safe in their brick house... Unlike what happens with actual bacon," Linda smiled.

"I could get used to this," Sarah smiled.

"Your breakfast is ready," Linda smiled. "You can also warm those muffins. The bakery next door has an amazing collection of vegan options, and those are my favorite. I am going for a shower. The milonga starts in a couple of minutes. It's the Saturday night milonga, so if you have any dress that you think is too much, this might be the night to wear it. The tiger-patterned heels are the right choice too."

Sarah looked at her, terrified. "I didn't bring any dress, just the heels."

Linda smiled and took her by the hand to her bedroom. She opened the wardrobe, and Sarah's mouth dropped open once again. "I told you I had more of those at home, right?"

Linda casually slipped out of her clothes and stepped into the shower, leaving the door open. "Enjoy your breakfast, Sarah. Those dresses aren't going anywhere," she called out, her voice echoing slightly against the tile.

"I don't think I have time. I want to try them all," said Sarah.

"There is not enough time in the world for that," Linda said. "Trust me, I tried."

Sarah finished off the scrambled eggs and bacon, then downed a full glass of fresh orange juice in one long gulp, and returned to Linda's room. She opened the wardrobe once again. She heard Linda getting out of the shower and a few seconds later the sound of a towel landing on the bed.

"Try the deep blue one. It'll match your shoes perfectly," Linda suggested from behind.

"This one?" Sarah pointed to the right and turned her head toward Linda.

Linda was naked, looking at three thongs lying in front of her on the bed. Sarah quickly turned her head toward the wardrobe.

"No, not that one," Linda said gently, placing her hands on Sarah's hips and guiding her a few steps back to reveal the dress she had in mind. "Come." She cradled it gently, bent at the waist, and carefully placed it on the bed.

"I don't know which one is sexier," Sarah smiled.

"That would be me," Linda said and stood up. She picked up her mobile and seconds later tango music filled the room. "Now put that on, while I am making the hardest decision of my night." She stared at the underwear one more time.

"Be right back," Sarah called out, her voice tinged with excitement. She delicately lifted the dress, the fabric whispering against her skin as she carried it to her room, each step filled with eager anticipation.

She closed her eyes and felt the fabric cascade through her fingers. Then, she lifted it overhead, slipping into the embrace of the bodice. The garment draped effortlessly down her figure as she adjusted the straps to sit on her shoulders. With a subtle shimmy, the dress fell into place. Sarah looked at herself over her shoulder in her wardrobe's mirror.

As Sarah admired her reflection, Linda breezed into the room. "And what a beautiful butt this is," she teased, giving Sarah an approving glance. Linda's red dress clung to her form, accentuating every curve with striking precision, and a deep V-neckline went all the way down, almost to her belly button.

Sarah noticed a shimmer on Linda's shoulders. "What's making your skin sparkle like that?" she asked, her curiosity piqued.

"It's my cream, I'll show you," Linda smiled. They both turned toward the mirror.

The dresses looked surprisingly similar, except for the color and a few details.

"You did that on purpose, didn't you?" Sarah said.

"All eyes will be on us, honey," Linda shook her shoulders. "Come, make-up time," she said and danced to her bathroom.

"I feel like I am getting ready for my high-school prom," Sarah said.

Linda chuckled softly. "My dad would've never let me out of the house in this for prom," she mused, a playful glint in her eyes. She poured a bit of cream on her hands, rubbed them, and gently spread it on Sarah's shoulders, massaging them.

"You are good at this," Sarah closed her eyes.

"I lived a year in Thailand, giving massages for a living."

"Is there somewhere you haven't traveled?"

"A couple of countries," Linda smiled. "My next tango trip is going to be in Greece. Next week."

"They dance tango there too?" Sarah asked, surprised.

"You have no idea," Linda responded with a huge smile on her face. "You should come."

"Yeah, right," she said, gently squeezing the eyelash curler. "As if Mark would ever say yes to that."

"If you don't ask, he won't say no either," Linda responded and looked at the bathroom clock. "Time to go."

Sarah smiled when she saw Linda's car. A vintage convertible, painted in a striking shade of deep red. She opened the door, and sat on the leather seat, that was worn just enough to feel lived-in. The only thing that seemed to be from the twenty-first century was the phone mount.

Linda inserted a CD and clicked 'play.' "Time to take flight," she declared with a flourish. As she pressed a button, the convertible's top smoothly retracted, filling the night air with the lilting strains of a tango vals.

As they drove, Linda seemed unfazed by the curious glances from passersby, her confidence unshakable. Sarah, feeling a tad more self-conscious, slid down in her seat just a little, her excitement mingling with a touch of shyness.

"Looks like they've never seen two princesses on their way to the ball," Linda quipped, her voice light and amused, as she effortlessly navigated through the traffic.

The drive to the milonga was a blur of city lights and tango music, with Linda's laughter punctuating the evening air. Sarah watched the streets pass by, her thoughts a mix of anticipation and nervous excitement. When they finally arrived, the familiar buzz of the milonga greeted them.

"Ah, the ladies gracing us just before midnight?" James said with a wide, welcoming smile, his tone playfully teasing.

"You know how it is, James. A woman faces tough decisions before stepping out, a world of choices in just one closet," Linda replied with a theatrical sigh.

"I am sure you made the best one. Your table, and Diego, await," James said, gesturing towards a spot in the room. Sarah followed his gaze.

As they stepped into the main venue, Sarah glanced at Linda. "So, which fabulous underwear did you end up choosing?" she asked playfully.

Linda responded with a sassy wink and a playful strut of her hips. "They were all so fabulous, I simply *couldn't* decide," she exclaimed and went off to greet a group of women standing next to the bar. Sarah walked toward her table laughing.

The sound of Sarah's laughter caught Diego's attention, prompting him to turn his head. His eyes briefly met hers before taking in her appearance, lingering momentarily on the V-neck and the elegant cut of her dress. His mouth opened. "You look absolutely stunning," he uttered standing up.

"Thank you," Sarah said. "Hug?"

Diego took a few steps closer and opened his arms. Sarah melted into his embrace, and they stayed there for what felt like a minute. Neither felt the need to end the embrace, and Diego showed no indication of wanting to stop.

Sarah smelled Diego's neck. "That smells amazing," she said, "what are you wearing?" She waited for a few seconds but no answer came back. She looked up into his eyes.

"I am not sure what you mean," he said.

"Your cologne, it smells great, like woods and spice."

Sarah saw Diego's expression change. He put his arms on her shoulders and took a small step back. He stared into her eyes without saying a word. His head tilted a bit to the right. She noticed his pupils becoming a tiny bit bigger and his eyes shinier. He looked up for a moment and then he closed his eyes. A tear went down his right cheek.

"I am sorry," Sarah said confused. "I meant it as a good thing." She put her hand on his cheek.

Diego let his head rest on her hand and a sad smile appeared on his face. "Don't be."

"What happened?" Sarah stepped closer to him.

"I am not wearing any cologne," said Diego.

Sarah looked confused. "So?"

"Only one person ever described my smell like this." Diego said. "I want to dance with you. Is that OK?"

"Sure, yes," Sarah said and pulled her heels out of the bag.

A minute later, she put her left hand around his neck and with the right she looked for his palm. Gently, his fingers traced the outline of her hand before guiding it to rest against his chest, where he covered it with his own hand. His heartbeat resonated beneath Sara's touch, robust and steady, each breath drawing her hand in. Adjusting her left hand on his neck, she gently gripped her fingers onto his chest with her right.

They moved slowly, together. Sarah felt a small spasm inside his embrace. A few seconds later, another one. Diego's head tilted a bit and Sarah lifted hers. She could now feel the air coming out of his mouth brushing her lips. Another spasm. She felt a warm tear sliding down her cheek. She used her fingers to caress his neck. One more tear. They breathed and moved, stepped and paused.

By the end of the song Diego had stopped crying. They stayed embraced.

"Who was she?" Sarah asked.

"A hurricane," Diego whispered.

"Do I feel like one?"

"You feel like home," Diego whispered.

"If you want to talk, I am here for you."

"Talking is overrated. I prefer this."

When the tanda finished, Linda and Jonathan were waiting for them. A bottle of wine and four empty glasses stood in a row, catching the flickering light of a candle. Jonathan stood up and embraced Sarah.

"When can we open this?" asked Diego.

"A red one for the gentleman is coming right up," Linda smiled and opened the bottle. "Wine?" She looked at Sarah.

Sarah nodded yes, and Linda filled all four glasses.

Linda raised her glass, her eyes twinkling. "So, what are we toasting to tonight?" she asked the group.

"To those who are there when we need them?" Sarah suggested.

Linda smiled. "All together, then." She raised her glass.

"To those who are there when we need them," they all chimed in, their voices mingling in a heartfelt, albeit slightly disjointed, chorus.

Sarah looked over her glass at Diego as he placed the glass to his lips. He closed his eyes and took a long drink, emptying the glass in one smooth motion.

"What are we celebrating?" a voice asked.

Sarah turned her head, and a huge smile appeared on her face.

"Maria!"

"Let me get you a glass," Diego offered warmly, quickly heading over to the bar.

Jonathan grabbed a nearby chair and placed it next to the table. Maria sat gracefully, adjusting her purple skirt.

Diego returned with a glass as the next tanda started. Linda gave him a look, and they excused themselves. Sarah's gaze drifted across the dance floor, watching the swirl of dancers.

"Looks like Linda worked her magic to bring you here," Maria said with a knowing smile.

"Shhh," Sarah whispered, placing her index finger in front of her mouth.

Jonathan didn't say a word and kept looking toward the dance floor.

Maria eyed Sarah's dress. "That looks like one of Linda's, doesn't it?"

"Yeah, I'm crashing at her place for a bit," Sarah confirmed, a hint of gratitude in her voice.

"Because of what happened in the class?"

"Because of tango."

"Jonathan, I think this young lady needs us," Maria said. "Problems with Mark, her boyfriend. What happened, honey?"

They listened to Sarah sharing about her fights with Mark. Every now and then, Maria asked a few questions, while Jonathan remained silent.

"What is it that really bothers you?" Maria asked at the end.

"Tango makes me feel things I never felt before," Sarah said. "I can't imagine myself without it. And Mark is a guy I can stay with for life, but life seems to just slip through our fingers and time is passing. I am getting older. Am I too selfish?"

"Believe me, honey, time has a way of slipping by faster than we ever imagine," Maria said, her voice tinged with a mix of wisdom and nostalgia. She looked at Jonathan who nodded with a smile. "Look, men think with their heads most of the time. We women, we lead with our hearts. You can't deny your feelings. You found something in tango that you were looking for. Don't you think there is a way to explain it to him in words that he understands? Perhaps there's a way to connect it to something he's passionate about. Does he have any hobbies or interests that might be a good analogy?" Maria suggested thoughtfully.

"His passion is his job," Sarah answered. "But I can already hear his response. 'Work is necessary, tango is not.' He won't get it."

"Did he ever dance or do something else outside of work?" Maria asked.

"When we first started dating, he was into classic cars. He's quite a good amateur mechanic, actually. He used to meet with his friends and restore old cars."

"Maybe you could remind him of that?" Maria said, looking at Jonathan for support.

Jonathan set his glass down thoughtfully. "The day before you tried tango," he began, his gaze drifting toward the dance floor, "were you happy?"

Sarah looked at the dancers in front of her. They appeared to be in their late seventies. The song was very fast, and the man was making mistakes every few steps. But the lady in his embrace kept laughing and moving on. "How do I get what they have?" Sarah asked.

"Say no more," Jonathan said and stood up. "Let's dance this milonga."

"That's the fast one, right? Diego hasn't taught me that yet," Sarah said.

"Just keep your steps small," Jonathan said, his smile reassuring as he gently led her onto the dance floor.

Chapter 17

The soft glow of dawn gradually spilled through the curtains, casting a gentle illumination on the room. Sarah, her eyelids heavy from unrest, stirred restlessly in her sleep. A few seconds later, she opened her eyes and looked straight at the ceiling. Despite the fatigue, a spark of energy and purpose flickered within. A few moments later, gently slipping out from the cozy embrace of her blankets, she tiptoed through the room and into the bathroom. With a few quiet splashes, she readied herself. She stepped carefully to avoid any noise and got dressed. As she passed next to Linda's half-opened door, she paused, listening to the rhythmic breathing within, finding a moment's solace in the steadiness it offered. Then, she took her shoes in her hands, grabbed her bag, and got out of the house.

She closed the door gently and turned around, pausing as a pair of startled birds flew away. The air was crisp and fresh, and the morning sun, breaking through the night's humidity, made the dew on Linda's flowers glisten. Sarah slipped on her shoes, slid into her car, and tossed her bag onto the passenger seat. The car's interior was cool, the leather seats holding the chill of the night. She typed 'Gramofon' and Eugen Doga's waltz appeared in the results. As the first piano notes filled the car, she turned the key and looked at herself in the mirror.

"It's time," she said, looking straight into her eyes.

The car glided through the desolate Sunday streets, with Sarah driving almost mechanically. As she turned into her street, she noticed the trees on the side. One, two, three... She finally eased the car into its usual spot. She looked at the mirror once more. "Seven."

Stepping through the street door, Sarah's gaze lingered on the beauty of her flowers, positioned outside the garden's neat grass lines. She approached the baby swing in the left corner. She kneeled and gave a gentle push on the swing. It wobbled front and back a few times before coming to a halt. She stood up, placed one hand on each post, and closed her eyes. After a deep breath, she went up the stairs and turned the key.

Stepping inside, the house greeted her with its familiar silence, broken only by the soft clinks and clatters of dishes from the kitchen. With her bag still on and the keys in her hands, she walked toward it.

Mark, absorbed in the task of emptying the dishwasher, stiffened for a moment as he caught sight of her. He stood up holding a few stacked dishes. They looked into each other's eyes silently for a few seconds. Then, he turned and placed the dishes slowly, one by one, on the shelf.

"You made a choice," he said, his voice barely above a whisper, still looking at the plates.

"I did." She looked down.

Mark picked a few more dishes from the dishwasher. "And you are sure it's the right one."

"It hurts. So I guess it is."

Mark's shoulders tensed. He continued putting dishes on the shelf. "So?"

Sarah remained silent for a few seconds. Her fingers moved. She placed the key on the kitchen table and the subtle clink seemed to reverberate through the room.

She saw the back of Mark's head as he looked toward the window.

She took a few steps closer. Mark didn't move.

"I am sorry," she said, her voice cracking. "It *does* hurt."

With a silent nod, Mark kept his gaze averted. Sarah slowly made her way through the hallway. She stepped outside and gently pulled the door until the bolt touched the frame. Tears traced warm paths down her cheeks, each breath drawn deep. At the end, she gave the final pull. The bolt extended into the frame with a clink. She lifted her head and looked at the bell on her right. She traced Mark's name with her finger.

One slow step at a time, she walked down the stairs and approached her flowers. She placed one hand gently on top of a rose, feeling the petal's coolness against her skin. She brought the fingers to her nose, and smelled the lingering fragrance. "Goodbye," she whispered. She took a few steps, then turned back and lifted a small pot of dwarf sunflowers that she had planted a few weeks ago. "You are coming with me."

She secured the pot on the front seat next to her and drove slowly away. *Seven*, she thought as the seventh tree appeared in her rearview mirror. *Six*. The empty street stared at her. *Five, Four.* "Come on," she whispered. *Three. Two.* "Come on." *One.* The last tree disappeared behind her. The street was still empty. She looked at her eyes, red and full of tears. "You better know what you are doing, young lady."

Arriving at Linda's, Sarah hesitated, her hand hovering over the doorbell. A glance at her watch made her decision. She turned away and headed to the local bakery. The welcoming smell of warm bread hit her nose.

"What are your vegan options?"

An old lady at the cashier took her order and placed everything inside brown paper bags. "This would be 23,50. And this one is from me," she said and placed a croissant in another bag. "It's with chocolate." She looked at her as a grandma looks at her grandchildren. "You look like you need it," the lady said with a sympathetic smile.

Sarah nodded. "Thank you."

She crossed the street, and rang the bell. A minute later Linda opened the door. She was just wearing her underwear and her hair was all over the place. "What's wrong with you?" she said and yawned. "We are not supposed to wake up for," she turned her head to check the clock in the living room, "another five hours at least."

Sarah lifted her right hand higher, showing the bags from the bakery.

"Any coffee in there?"

Sarah nodded.

"Good. Get in. Why did you wake up so early?"

Sarah walked inside and lifted her other hand. Linda stared at the sunflower for a few seconds. "You brought me flowers?"

"No," said Sarah with a sigh.

Linda gasped and leaned forward. "Oh dear. Are you OK?"

"No," Sarah said, tears running once again. Her knees weakened and she started collapsing. The bags and the flower fell on the floor. Linda managed to catch her at the last moment. She lifted her up in the air and carried her into the bedroom.

She placed her on the bed and took her clothes off. Sarah rolled under the covers. She curled up like a baby, crying and shaking. Linda came from the other side and hugged her from behind. Sarah felt Linda's warm skin on her. She took her hand and placed it on her diaphragm.

"Oh dear," Linda said as Sarah's body shook. "It's OK, let it out. I am here, we'll pass this together."

Sarah squeezed Linda's hand on her and cried until she fell asleep.

Chapter 18

When she woke up, she found herself in Linda's embrace. Her face was laying on Linda's chest.

"Good evening," Linda said smoothly and stroked Sarah's hair. "How long have I been sleeping?"

"Four hours."

"And you stayed here?"

"I couldn't leave even if I wanted to," Linda said and pointed down.

Sarah's left leg was wrapped all around Linda's legs, with her thighs resting on her abdomen.

"Sorry, I get cold when I sleep," Sarah smiled.

"It's fine with me," Linda said. "But I am starving. Let's eat?"

"I don't want to get out of bed," Sarah said.

"You don't need to," Linda smiled and tried to stand up. "May I?" she said after a failed attempt, pointing at Sarah's leg.

"I'll be cold," Sarah smiled.

"I'll be back in five minutes, I promise," Linda said.

Sarah watched Linda as she walked away. She heard the familiar beep of the microwave a few times.

Linda came back with a tray carrying toasted bread, croissants, coffee, and blueberry muffins. "Don't you love the smell of breakfast in the afternoon?" she smiled. She got under the covers and came close to Sarah. "Shall we?" she smiled, looking at the muffins.

They each grabbed one and took a bite at the same time. In synchrony, they let out a soft sigh of delight.

"Better than sex," Sarah said.

"Only if you are not doing it right," Linda said, and they burst into laughter.

"How did you manage to lift me up in the air before?" Sarah asked. "I didn't realize you were so strong."

"I," she paused and took a deep breath. Her eyes closed. "I had a lot of practice."

Sarah put her muffin down and looked at her.

"I had a son. He was diagnosed with Duchenne. He already couldn't walk by the age of nine. The muscles. And then a complication appeared."

Sarah put her arms around Linda.

"We fell asleep together many times here."

Sarah felt her eyes welling up with tears. "Linda, I... I didn't know."

"I hadn't slept in this bed for years."

Sarah wiped away some tears from Linda's face. "I am here for you. Whatever you need."

Linda fought back her tears and forced a laugh. "I need my muffin." She took a big bite.

Sarah lifted her muffin too. "I think we need something stronger than that," Sarah said. "Tell me about Greece."

Chapter 19

Sarah placed a pack of paper boxes in front of Mark's front door and rang the bell. Samantha, the cleaning lady, answered. Her hazel eyes exuded a kindness that always put Sarah at ease. Of average height with a sturdy build, her red hair was always neatly tied in a ponytail for practicality.

"Sarah, it's good to see you," Samantha said, her face lighting up with a warm smile. "I'm really sorry to hear about everything. Are you holding up okay?"

"It's hard. Is Mark here?" Sarah whispered.

"No. Can I help you?" Samantha asked.

Sarah sighed in relief. "I could certainly use a hand," she said. "It would be great if I could leave before..."

"Say no more. Let's start with the bedroom?" Samantha suggested, grabbing two boxes and moving with a gentle grace born from years of familiarity with the house.

As they entered the bedroom, Sarah noticed the absence of the red carpet.

"Mark decided to have the carpet cleaned professionally," Samantha explained while gently folding Sarah's clothes on the bed. "I told him a bit of ammonia would do the trick, but he wouldn't have it."

"Let's focus on the task at hand," Sarah said, moving with quiet determination. The familiar scent of lavender mingled with the sharp aroma of packing tape as they worked silently side by side. Sarah's fingers lingered over a worn-out t-shirt, a relic from a lazy Sunday morning.

She navigated the shelves that once cradled their shared stories. Books were carefully stacked, their titles telling tales of shared passions. A framed photograph caught her eye, a frozen moment of smiles now feeling like echoes from another time. Sarah hesitated before gently placing it into a box.

The sound of tape being pulled and stretched filled the room. Items from their shared life were now reduced to their material essence, ready to be boxed. Sarah carefully wrapped a porcelain mug, one of Mark's first gifts when they moved in, and packed it in the corner of a box.

Samantha worked diligently, offering occasional empathetic glances. As the boxes filled, Sarah's movements became both deliberate and tender. Samantha helped carry each box into the car.

The final box sealed, Sarah stood in the doorway.

Samantha's voice, soft and hesitant, broke the silence. "Did it really have to be this way?"

A glistening moisture gathered at the corners of Sarah's eyes. "No," Sarah said, "it didn't."

Samantha took Sarah's hands in her own. "What's your plan now, Sarah?"

"I'm heading to Athens tomorrow."

Samantha looked at her surprised. "For how long?"

"I don't know."

"What about your job at the hospital?"

The question hung in the air. Sarah's response was a mere whisper, "I've left it behind, just like everything else."

"But why, Sarah? I don't understand," Samantha said.

"Neither do I," Sarah responded. "At least, not yet." Sarah paused. "How is he?"

"He's been really down, Sarah. I've never seen him like this. I think you should talk. Trust me."

Sarah gave a small smile. "I wish it was that simple. Samantha, thank you for everything. You've been a blessing to us." She hugged her and got in the car. As she drove away, she took a last look in the mirror, seeing Samantha waving goodbye.

Linda was waiting for her at the front door and ran down once she saw her parking. "How did it go?"

"Mark wasn't there, that made things easier."

Linda helped her carry the boxes back into her room.

"Do you feel ready to unpack and then pack for the trip?" Linda asked.

Sarah collapsed face-first onto the bed. "I don't think I can go through this again today."

"I thought you would say that," Sarah said. "Unfortunately, you don't have that option. So..."

A few seconds later, the sound of percussion instruments, violin, and a few other instruments Sarah couldn't recognize filled the room. She turned her head to the side and opened one eye.

"What's that?"

"Ikariotikos," Linda read the title. "It's Greek music. Now, where are your sundresses?"

Sarah looked at the stacked boxes. "The one on the bottom left," she said, grateful to Samantha for remembering to label them. "What's with all the shouting in the song?"

"I have no idea," Linda said, looking at her mobile. "But they seem to be having a lot of fun." She turned the screen toward Sarah. A few hundred people were dancing with their hands on each other's shoulders, big smiles on their faces, and whistling every now and then.

"I want what they are having," Sarah smiled.

"Did you see these guys here?" Linda pointed at three tall guys dancing at the front of the line. They all had short black hair, broad shoulders, and big smiles on their faces. "The monuments are waiting. Get your beautiful butt out of the bed and let's get ready."

"I thought we were going for tango," Sarah said and stood up.

"I am sure some monuments dance tango too," Linda smiled. "I joined some Facebook groups in Athens. There are milongas every day, sometimes more than one. Tomorrow night is supposed to be a very good one."

Sarah looked at Linda. "Thank you, I need this."

Chapter 20

"Ladies and gentlemen, we have begun our descent into Athens. Please turn off all portable electronic devices..."

Sarah tuned out the announcement, her gaze irresistibly drawn to the window. As the sprawling cityscape of Athens unfolded below, a mix of anticipation and uncertainty fluttered in her chest. So, this is where the next chapter begins, she thought, her heart skipping a beat at the newness of it all. The sun was setting behind them, painting the whole sky in shades of red, orange, and pink. She marveled at how the blue sea kissed the narrow coastline, giving way to an endless mosaic of white buildings. A few well-lit large straight lines indicated the main avenues, with houses chaotically distributed among thousands of intersecting small streets. She tingled with excitement at the prospect of exploring these streets.

"Should we eat something when we arrive?" Linda asked.

"I am still full. The food was delicious," Sarah replied, looking at the Aegean Airlines logo in front of her.

"They say Greek food is amazing," Linda mused, her eyes sparkling with anticipation.

A white building on a hill caught Sarah's attention, bathed in lights from all directions. It was surrounded by a huge wall, with trees and occasional white structures dotting the area around it.

"Look, there is the Acropolis, right there!" Sarah said, her voice tinged with childlike excitement.

"What a surprise," Linda smiled. "Do you see any monuments?"

"Nothing that moves yet," Sarah chuckled, and they both laughed.

"Do you see that little semicircle on the side of the hill?" Linda pointed out the window. "Our apartment is close to that."

"I have no sense of direction without my GPS," Sarah admitted, "and you can find our apartment in a city you haven't even visited yet?"

"Let's hope you don't get lost then," Linda teased.

Sarah smiled softly, her gaze lingering on the cityscape. "I kind of want to," she confessed.

Once they landed and gathered their luggage, Sarah and Linda found themselves in a taxi departing from the bustling airport terminal. The vibrant life of the city, so different from her own, stirred a curious blend of exhilaration and nostalgia within her. The driver navigated effortlessly through the bustling streets, occasionally revealing glimpses of hills in the distance. Approaching the city center, Sarah observed the lively street life with people strolling, and the presence of shops, cafes, and restaurants. Colorful graffiti adorned some of the buildings along the route. The final stretch of their drive took them through narrow, winding streets, flanked by traditional historic buildings.

When they finally arrived, Linda led the way up a narrow, cobblestone path to their rented apartment. With an excited flourish, she swung open the door.

Sarah stepped into a world that seemed like a perfect blend of past and present. She felt a sudden longing, a connection to something she couldn't quite name, as she ran her fingers over the smooth, cool surfaces of their temporary home. Street light spilled through the windows, casting a warm orange glow on the room. The walls were adorned with local artwork and vibrant colors. A small bottle and a box of sweets were on the kitchen table.

"Ouzo," Sarah said, looking at the label. "Forty-five percent alcohol."

"Now we are talking," Linda approached with a little hop.

Moving further into the apartment, they discovered the bedrooms, each with neatly made beds and soft, inviting linens. The walls, adorned with delicate frescoes of olive groves and the Aegean Sea, created an ambiance of tranquil Greek idyll. Music drifted in through the windows. Sarah approached and leaned out slightly, drinking in the view. The sight of the Acropolis in the distance filled her with a sense of adventure.

"Do you think we can be ready in twenty minutes? I can't wait to go out," Sarah said.

"Absolutely," Linda responded and opened her luggage.

"What will you wear?" Sarah asked.

Linda's eyes sparkled with mischief. "It's our first milonga here. I say we give them something to remember," she proposed, her voice laced with excitement.

"I was thinking of going low profile tonight, see how they are dressed first," Sarah said.

"You do you, honey, I do me."

The air felt warm as they got out of the house half an hour later. They walked down the street and hailed a taxi.

"It seems there are more taxis here than normal cars," Sarah observed, pointing at many yellow cars passing by.

"Take us to Monstraki, please," Linda said to the driver, a middle-aged man with a beard.

"Monastiraki you mean?" he responded with a strong accent.

Linda took another look at her mobile and nodded, "Yes, please."

"What two beautiful ladies like you do here? Vacations eh?" the driver asked.

"We came to dance tango," Linda said.

"Tango? You professionals?"

"Not really," Linda said, "just a hobby."

"I had a girlfriend. Beautiful woman. From Argentina. We loved a lot. She didn't dance. But she sang songs, beautiful songs."

"What happened to her?" Linda inquired.

"She couldn't stay. No papers, couldn't find work. She went back," he said, a hint of sadness in his voice. "But she left me this." He pulled a CD out of a case and pushed it into the CD player.

Sarah loved the sound of Spanish lyrics, even though she couldn't understand them. She looked outside as the piano notes accompanied the woman's voice.

"One day she'll come back," he said once the song finished.

"Why don't you go there?" Linda asked.

The driver lifted his right hand and rubbed the thumb against the tips of his index and middle fingers. "Money. Not enough. And if I go there, what will I do? I don't speak Spanish. We arrived, Monastiraki. I leave you here or more down?"

Linda lifted her mobile and pointed at the screen with the address.

"I leave you here. I don't drive in small streets. Too many people. I enter, we take twenty minutes to get there. You walk, you are there in three."

He parked the car next to some big garbage bins. "Go straight. Third street, turn left, it's there."

Tiny restaurants lined both sides of the street, each one with its own personality and music. Linda pointed at the drawing of a big Cuban flag next to a bar. People were dancing salsa inside. "Maybe after?" she suggested.

A few steps later, they heard different kinds of Greek music coming from bars and restaurants. Tables were on the street, with the occasional car slowly passing a hair's breadth from the chairs. In some cases, the patrons had to move a bit for the car to fit. People were chatting loudly to hear each other above the music.

Sarah pointed up. A sign on the first floor above a restaurant read 'Tango Studio.'

"Do you see any entrance?" Sarah asked.

"No, but I know who'll take us there," Linda pointed at a couple walking near them. The man was wearing baggy pants and the woman was carrying a shiny green shoe bag.

They followed them and found the entrance tucked away on a quieter street. Ascending the stairs to the first floor, the faint sound of tango music began to fill the air. On the right, a smiley girl seated next to a table welcomed them.

"Kalispera," she said.

"Hi," Linda smiled, "good evening."

"Welcome to El Cabeceo. The milonga has just started. Two tickets?"

Linda nodded.

"You have one free drink each, and you can sit wherever you want. I recommend sitting on the right side, though, most couples form there. Open the door slowly, it opens right into the dance floor."

"Thank you," Linda said, her hand gently pushing the door open.

They walked along the side of the dance floor and settled onto a gold couch adorned with gold pillows. Black and gold chairs were strategically positioned around the dance floor. The ceiling featured large squares concealing hidden lighting. In the center of these squares, white and gracefully curved lines formed patterns resembling flowers. The entire venue was surrounded by windows that overlooked the bustling streets Sarah and Linda had strolled along earlier. Red curtains partially covered some of the windows, casting a dim glow from outside and creating a striking contrast to the black walls.

The DJ, a bold guy with a piercing in his left eyebrow, chatted cheerfully with a couple of young guys seated next to him. Sarah looked at five couples already dancing. The steps they were doing were simple, but their posture was straight and elegant. Each couple maintained a respectful distance from each other.

"Did you see the trophies?" Sarah said while putting on her heels.

Linda looked at the wall behind the couch. Two big trophies and a gold laurel wreath were in the middle, surrounded by photographs from a competition and of people dancing, as well as a framed newspaper article.

"There are tango competitions every year around the world. The biggest one is in Buenos Aires."

An upbeat tune reverberated through the room. Sarah looked back at the guys. One of them stood out. Average height, with neatly cropped short hair and what looked like a tailor-made tango suit, he was paying attention silently to what his friend was saying. He said a few words and then fell silent again. His eyes caught Sarah looking at him. He smiled and Sarah smiled back. As he moved toward her, there was a subtle bounce in his step, reminiscent of a happy child walking inside his favorite toy store. He smiled at Sarah with a gleaming set of perfect teeth.

"Good evening," he said, his voice carrying a warm, hospitable tone that seemed characteristic of the locals. "You seem new to our city. If you need any guidance or have questions, please don't hesitate to ask. I'm Vaggelis."

"I am Sarah, and this is Linda. It looks beautiful. I love those flowers on the ceiling. And the people here seem to dance so elegantly." She pointed at the couples.

"They are from the beginners' class. It finishes right before the milonga, so they stay afterward and dance."

"They are *beginners*?"

"The focus here is on creating a nice embrace and a comfortable walk right from the beginning. They might not know many steps yet, but they're learning the soul of tango. It makes everything easier later."

"If *they* dance like this, I can't imagine how their teacher dances," Sarah said.

"She is amazing. Her partner needs to improve," Vaggelis said.

"Would you mind introducing us to some locals?" Linda asked.

"Absolutely," he said. "But would you mind if I asked your friend for a dance first? I like this song."

Sarah walked toward the dance floor, only to notice that no one else was dancing. People were still chatting, and some of them were looking at her. For a moment, she felt grateful she hadn't followed Linda's example. Her pale blue dress, with simple clean lines, was not there to draw attention. She lifted her hand and a delicate bracelet slid down her wrist.

Vaggelis waited for her to embrace him. His embrace closed, allowing Sarah to keep her embrace as she wanted. He waited a few beats, softly changing the weight a couple of times. Then, he led a perfectly timed to the music side step. Sarah felt that she had no option but to step exactly where he indicated. As they continued moving, his leading was so clear that she had no doubt about what she should do and when. Each step was calm and confident. Sarah found herself doing steps that were longer than her usual and felt much more stable. They alternated between soft, slow sequences and energetic and explosive ones. Sarah kept her eyes closed until the song finished.

She felt a bit disappointed when Vaggelis opened the embrace. *What's the point of talking when you can dance?* She found herself in front of a mirror that covered half the wall.

"I love this milonga," she smiled and pretended to check herself in the mirror.

110

Vaggelis watched her with a soft, appreciative smile. His gaze suggested a man who found true joy in the happiness of others.

Sarah embraced him one more time, as a new song began with a melodic whisper. A few seconds later, the music intensified as the rhythmic pulse of the double bass and the bandoneon established a heartbeat. The violins, with their rich resonance, added a layer of drama. The bandoneon became more assertive, engaging in a musical dialogue with the piano. Sarah felt a sense of urgency and anticipation as their movements echoed the rise and fall of the instruments. The music built towards a climactic moment, and then the bandoneon reached its zenith, urging them into a series of fast movements. The violins soared, and the piano added flourishes that Vaggelis caught and incorporated into Sarah's steps. As the final notes lingered, the music slowed down, and Sarah felt his embrace becoming softer. They melted into each other's arms as the final note hit.

As Sarah opened her eyes she saw they were in front of the couch again. Not sure what to say, she looked again at the pictures on the wall. Looking at the couple holding the trophy, Sarah was taken aback.

"Hey, that's you," she said.

"That was ten years ago," he said, "it was a beautiful event."

"So that's your milonga. And that makes you the teacher too, right?"

Vaggelis nodded.

"Is your partner here?"

"Marianna. Yes, she is dancing with your friend."

Sarah saw Linda dancing with a woman who looked to be about the same height as Vaggelis. She had big, expressive lips and deep black eyes. Her black hair framed her face. Despite her thin body, she boasted an exquisite silhouette, accentuated by a sculpted back and enviable curves. She moved with a captivating blend of strength and grace. The dance was a beautiful exchange of energy. Marianna translated Linda's lead into a seamless and fluid response. At one moment the boundaries between leader and follower blurred, and the next moment they simultaneously repositioned their arms with a smile. Marianna was now the leader, as they moved gracefully toward the other end of the dance floor. Linda, a living canvas of extravagance, twirled in a flamboyant dress that seemed to capture the essence of a tropical sunset. The fabric burst with passionate reds, vibrant oranges, and lively yellows. Ruffled layers cascaded down the skirt, creating a mesmerizing play of movement with every step. A statement necklace adorned her neck. As Linda spun, her voluminous skirt fanned out like a kaleidoscope.

"Do you lead too?" Vaggelis asked.

"Not yet."

"Do you want to learn?" he asked, and something in his tone showed he was genuinely interested in knowing.

"They seem to have so much fun," she said as Linda and Marianna once again changed roles. "I feel it could help me understand the follower's role better. You know what, yes, I would love to learn," she said with a smile.

Vaggelis nodded and they embraced again. When the tanda finished, he accompanied her to the couch. Linda came over with a huge smile.

"So, what can we drink around here?" she asked.

"Let me show you what we have at the bar," Vaggelis said.

Linda put her arm around his, winked at Sarah, and walked away.

Sarah sat on the couch and looked across the dance floor. Two tall guys were looking at her. She smiled at one of them and stood up for another dance.

As the hours passed, the atmosphere in the room transformed. What started as an energetic burst of music and movement had evolved into a more intimate ambiance. Sarah sat on the couch and took off her heels. Linda did the same a tanda later, and pulled a foot roller out of her bag. She smiled with pleasure as she rolled her feet on it.

"We have to buy you one of these," she said. "It seems we are going to need them here."

A young dancer approached them and looked at Linda. Linda lifted her head and, once he realized he was inviting her to dance, she lifted her bare foot in the air. The guy smiled and turned toward

Sarah. Sarah did the same. He shrugged his shoulders and walked away.

"Don't you feel really special when you are someone's second choice?" Linda said playfully to Sarah. "I don't understand how some guys don't seem to get that."

"Maybe he is a beginner," Sarah said.

"This has nothing to do with tango," Linda insisted. "This is basic social skills. I bet you he is not a good dancer."

Sarah looked at him as he approached one of the beginners she saw earlier that night. The woman smiled at him and stood up. It took a couple of seconds for the smile on her face to disappear.

"This is going to hurt," Linda said. "Poor girl."

Sarah watched the woman take a few steps and then lose her balance. She recovered, but she looked confused. The man seemed to be pushing her around. After a while, he pulled her toward him and opened his right leg to the side. The woman seemed even more confused. The guy whispered something in her ear, and the woman did a gancho, like the one Jessica had taught Sarah in the class. Step after step, the woman's confusion grew. When the song ended, Sarah breathed out. The woman thanked the guy and walked back to her seat.

Linda gave a look to Sarah, and they both stared at the guy walking right behind the woman. He stood in front of her and started talking. Then he projected his hand forward, inviting her to come back to the dance floor. The woman shook her head left and right. The man persisted for a few more seconds and then went back to his seat.

"The signals are all there if you know what to look for," said Linda. "And right now, if I were you, I would put my heels on and look to the left. A monument is trying to dance with you."

Sarah looked to her left and saw a tall man with broad shoulders and a lean physique looking at her. "What about the guy we just said no to, supposedly because we had taken our shoes off?"

"Are you going to say no to your happiness because of someone's inability to acquire social skills? By the way, I think I can see his abs through his suit," she said and laughed.

Sarah smiled at him and picked up her heels. He approached and waited patiently for her to put them on. As she looked at him, two dark eyes stared back. His black hair framed a confident face, and a chiseled jawline added a touch of rugged allure. His tango suit accentuated the contours of his physique, fitting tightly around his arms. He lifted his left hand. Sarah noticed a tattoo of a hunter on his wrist, holding a club and attacking a scorpion, just as she placed her hand on his.

Every movement he made on the dance floor was deliberate and precise. He stepped exactly where he needed to make Sarah move effortlessly around him. His lead was firm yet gentle, and nothing in his movement felt unnecessary. Sarah could feel his back creating a strong wall, and his posture was straight. His neck felt strong under Sarah's hand, and as they moved, she felt the little hair on his neck, indicating he had a haircut recently. And then, she felt it. The gentle void in his chest welcomed her in. She breathed in, and with an exhale, she offered her own void. She felt his posture softening a bit, allowing his head to tilt forward and turn a bit more toward her face. Sarah lifted her head slightly and placed her cheek on his. She felt the warmth coming out of his lips and a current ran through her spine. He slowed down their dance, until they came to an almost complete halt. Sarah accentuated her breathing, allowing her chest to move up and down. Without delay, he mirrored it. They breathed together for a few more notes, and as the final note hit their ears, Sarah lifted one leg and placed her inner thigh on the side of his hip.

Sarah didn't break the embrace and neither did he. They continued breathing. A few notes into the next song, Sarah slowly lowered her leg, caressing his, until her feet were back together again. With a common deep breath, they started moving again. Sarah could sense her heart beating stronger. She had no doubt he could feel it since she could feel his heartbeats too.

When the tanda finished, they stayed embraced for a few more seconds. Then Sarah took a step back, slowly sliding her left hand down his arm until she reached his fingers. He lowered her right hand while still holding it. His dark eyes closed, he took a deep breath in, and as he exhaled, he looked at her, squeezed her hands

114

a bit, and smiled at her. His smile was kind, and his head tilted slightly to the side. Then, he walked away.

"What just happened?" she said as she sat next to Linda.

"From where I was standing, it seems like you had *the* tanda. Was he smart? Please tell me he was smart. I can't even start counting how many times I had a great tanda and then they open their mouth and the whole thing goes straight to the garbage."

"He didn't talk."

"He is changing his shoes."

"What? Why?" Sarah asked and looked toward him.

"Would you want to dance with anyone else tonight after this tanda?"

"No."

"Neither does he. How did it feel?"

"Breaths and heartbeats," Sarah said.

"Some leaders make you take steps," Linda said, "some others make you feel things."

Sarah noticed the man walking toward the door. He was wearing a pair of white sneakers that were in total contrast with the suit above them. Without thinking about it, she stood up and followed him outside the door.

"Wait," Sarah called out, her voice tinged with a mix of hesitation and hope, as he was descending the stairs.

He looked at her.

Sarah tilted her head. "Are you leaving?" she asked, her voice carrying a note of disappointment.

He hesitated for a few seconds. "I could stay a while longer," he said and walked up the stairs.

The door opened once again, and a couple got out. Sarah and the man pressed their backs against the wall to let them pass.

"Come with me," he said and pointed toward the stairs going to the second floor. Sarah followed him. He stopped when they reached the top and sat on the stairs. She sat next to him.

"Did I cross any limits?" she asked.

He looked into her eyes, his gaze earnest. "I wouldn't change anything," he responded sincerely, a softness in his voice.

115

"What happened there?"

"You felt it, right?"

"Even my friend felt it," Sarah responded.

"A hundred hugs to find the one," he said and held her hand.

"A hundred hugs to find the one," Sarah whispered with a smile.

They stayed silent for a while, their fingers intertwined.

He leaned in slightly, his expression turning thoughtful. "Till when are you planning to stay?"

"I don't know yet. I don't have a return ticket."

"Will you go out to dance tomorrow?"

"Will you?" she smiled.

"I was hoping I could go on a date tomorrow," he said.

A frown creased Sarah's forehead. "Oh, you have a girlfriend," she said and pulled her hand away.

"No," he smiled. "Do you like Greek food?"

Sarah laughed. "I only tried the one on the airplane, I love it."

He took her hand in his again.

"Tomorrow at 8? We can meet downstairs. I know a great little restaurant. Some people say that the food there is even better than airplane food."

Sarah's lips curled into a playful smirk. "Do they serve peanuts and water in a tiny cup?"

"Don't be too exquisite."

"I'll do my best." Sarah winked at him and stood up. "See you tomorrow." She walked down the stairs and into the milonga. Linda was waiting for her with a big smile. "He asked me on a date tomorrow."

"Less than six hours in Greece and you are already ditching me?" asked Linda playfully.

"What can I do to make it up to you?" Sarah said, extending her arms to embrace Linda.

Linda lifted her hand, blocking her. "You'll need to give me all the spicy details when you're back from your date," she teased, a mischievous glint in her eye. "I always wondered how accurate the Greek statues are."

Chapter 21

"Vaggelis asked me if I want to learn how to lead," Sarah said, looking at her wardrobe.

"Why don't you take some classes with him? And try the yellow one next," Linda suggested.

"Do you think I'm ready to learn how to lead?" Sarah asked, taking off her skirt.

"If it were up to me, everyone would learn how to lead and follow from the first class."

"Wouldn't that be confusing?" Sarah wondered, pulling a yellow jumpsuit off a hanger.

"The two roles aren't so different. Both dancers need to know how to move their body, understand the geometry of the movement, and communicate through the embrace. The main difference is who initiates the movement."

"What about embellishments? You said I can do them when *I* decide." Sarah stepped into the jumpsuit and pulled it up.

"OK, the main difference is who *usually* initiates the movement, unless you're one of those followers who prefers to be led around without knowing what she is doing." Linda glanced at Sarah's outfit. "Is that an open-back?"

"Yes," Sarah replied, turning around for Linda to see.

"Hello, gorgeous," Linda complimented. "Your butt looks amazing."

"Thank you, I got it from my mama," Sarah joked, checking her watch. "I don't have much time. Is this too bold for a first date?"

"I don't think you're asking the right person," Linda smiled. "So, you're planning to arrive on time? You won't make him wait a bit?"

"I don't know his name, I don't have his phone number. If I'm late and he leaves, what then?"

"If he likes you, he'll wait. Let him prove it."

"Or I can just be on time and avoid the drama," Sarah decided and headed into the bathroom.

"He's Greek, they invented drama," Linda called out after her.

Twenty minutes later, Sarah stepped into the taxi, feeling the city's energy pulsating around her, adding an extra skip to her heartbeat with the excitement of the evening ahead.

"Monastiraki," she told the driver.

The driver nodded and began to navigate the labyrinth of Athens' streets. Soon, they encountered a sea of red brake lights, and the taxi came to a halt.

Sarah leaned forward, her forehead creasing slightly. "I guess driving in Athens is always an adventure, huh?" she said, her tone a mix of curiosity and mild frustration.

The driver chuckled. "Athens has a mind of its own sometimes. The problem today is the demonstration."

Sarah peered out the window and saw a police officer directing the traffic. "Is this going to delay us a lot? I need to be there in less than five minutes."

"No way," the driver said calmly. "By car, we'll need about twenty-five minutes if we're lucky. But I can get you to the beginning of Agion Asomaton Street in ten minutes, then you can walk the rest from there."

"Whatever is faster," Sarah agreed, checking her watch.

The driver swiftly turned into a side street, weaving through the traffic. Sarah gripped the door handle.

"Is this too fast for you?" he asked, glancing at her in the rearview mirror.

"You can't go fast enough," Sarah urged.

Minutes later, the driver pulled over, engaging the alarm lights. "That'll be eight fifty."

Sarah handed him a ten. "How do I get there?" she asked as drivers honked behind them.

"Just walk straight up this street. It'll lead you to Monastiraki," he instructed.

Stepping out, Sarah was immediately engulfed in the sounds of the bustling city. She sprinted down the pavement, quickly transitioning to a brisk walk. Rounding a curve past a small church, she spotted the familiar garbage bins, reassuring herself she wasn't lost. Glancing at her watch, she quickened her pace, feeling a bead of sweat trickle

118

down her back. Spotting the Tango Studio sign, she paused to catch her breath, aware of the curious glances from nearby patrons. She checked her watch again, more to signal her lateness than to tell the time.

She shifted her weight from one foot to the other, her gaze darting along the bustling streets, hoping to catch a glimpse of him.

"Crap," she muttered a bit too loudly a few seconds later, before turning to walk away.

"Did you go for a run?" a familiar voice called out from behind her.

Vaggelis was standing close by, a hint of amusement in his eyes.

"Hi, what are you doing here?" Sarah asked, slightly flustered.

Vaggelis gestured towards the sign. "I work here, remember? Can I help you with something?" he asked in his familiar friendly tone.

Sarah hesitated for a moment. "This is kind of embarrassing. Do you by any chance remember a tall guy, broad shoulders, black eyes at the milonga yesterday?"

"The one with the great embrace?" he asked, his smile growing.

"Yes, how did you know?" she asked, curious.

"I just assumed," he replied with a chuckle. "That would be Alexis."

"We were supposed to meet here half an hour ago. But I was late, and I don't have his number," Sarah admitted, her cheeks coloring slightly.

Vaggelis chuckled as he unlocked his phone. "In Greece, being half an hour late is just fashionably on time. I'll call him, he should be around. He's a remarkable dancer right? Been through a lot, but he keeps dancing. There's power in that... Alexis, hey, where are you?"

Sarah looked on, puzzled as to why Vaggelis was speaking English.

"A lady in yellow is looking for you. She said she has been waiting here for half an hour," Vaggelis winked at her.

Sarah smiled, placing her hands on her chest and mouthed 'thank you.'

"I think I can delay her for ten more minutes, but I can't make any promises," he said before ending the call.

"He's parking the car now. Athens is a mess tonight. Would you like to wait upstairs?"

119

They ascended the stairs and entered the studio. Sarah saw five women and Marianna practicing their embellishments.

"Why don't you join the class till Alexis arrives?" he suggested.

All the women turned their heads. "Alexis asked somebody out?" Marianna asked, clearly surprised.

"Enjoy the dance," Vaggelis told Sarah before hurrying off toward the mini-bar.

Sarah left her bag on a chair and joined the other women.

"Ena, dio, tria, tessera, ke..." All the women began moving forward in unison, and Sarah tried to mimic their movements.

"One step forward, one projection to the side, another step forward, another projection," the teacher instructed.

A few minutes later, the door opened, and Alexis entered, wearing jeans and a leather jacket. Sarah waved at him, and he returned her smile before heading to the mini-bar to greet Vaggelis. Sarah hesitated, wondering if she should leave the class but ultimately decided to stay.

Through the mirror, Sarah caught Alexis's gaze, lingering with an intensity that stirred a mix of nervousness and excitement within her. Each step she took felt more self-conscious, knowing his eyes followed her movements. His gaze seemed to explore, not just her movements, but something deeper. He was looking for something.

"Let's do some steps back, going around the floor," the teacher instructed.

As Sarah moved backward, away from Alexis, she felt his gaze on her. Turning her back to him, she became acutely aware of the open-back of her jumpsuit. Linda's words echoed in her mind, *your butt looks amazing*. With each backward step, she drew closer to where Alexis stood.

Finally, she turned around. Alexis had shifted his gaze to the window, leaning slightly against the wall, a plastic water cup in his hand, appearing tiny against his broad frame.

As the class came to an end, Sarah grappled with a whirlwind of emotions. The intensity of Alexis's gaze left her both exposed and intrigued. Gathering her belongings, she stole a glance at Alexis, who was engaged in conversation with Vaggelis. She straightened her

120

jumpsuit, took a deep breath to steady herself, and walked towards the door, ready for whatever the evening might bring.

They stepped out of the studio and ventured into a lively Athenian street.

"I am terribly sorry for the delay," Alexis apologized.

"You owe me one," Sarah said with a playful smile.

"I owe you one," he agreed, his own smile mirroring hers. "Are you hungry?"

"With all these aromas around us? How can I not be?" Sarah replied, her senses already captivated by the scents wafting through the air.

"Wonderful. Before we decide, is there anything you don't eat?" Alexis inquired.

Sarah shook her head. "No, I'm pretty open to trying new things."

"Great, because we've arrived," Alexis pointed to a restaurant to their left. The tables, set along the pedestrian street, were adorned with colorful cloths featuring whimsical designs of sausages, garlic, cheese, and red peppers. A large mural of a rooster added charm to the window. Patrons sat chatting at nearby tables, their laughter blending with the clinking of glasses.

Alexis stepped inside briefly and returned with an English menu. "I assume you haven't had time to learn Greek yet."

Sarah stood tall, a hint of pride in her voice. "Ena, dio, tria, tessera, ke..." She then glanced at the menu, her eyes widening. "Wow, there are so many choices!"

"Do you want to order the Greek way or the tourist way?" Alexis asked, a twinkle in his eye.

"The Greek way, please," Sarah responded eagerly.

"Then let's share a variety of small plates. I recommend the oven-baked feta with honey and sesame seeds, French fries, dolmadakia, domatokeftedes, and marathopita." He flipped the page. "There's also a fantastic Greek-style kebab, made with lamb and beef. How does that sound?"

Sarah beamed at him. "All of them sound amazing."

Alexis signaled for the waiter, and Sarah listened intently as he ordered in rapid Greek, the language flowing like a melodic stream.

She was able to catch a few words, like 'feta' and 'tzatziki', but everything else felt like a fast continuous buzz of sounds.

"You know, Greek sounds a bit like Spanish," Sarah observed.

"Yes, many people say the accents are similar. Now," Alexis leaned in, his gaze intense, "who are you?"

Sarah laughed. "Where do I start?"

"Start with why you are here."

Sarah looked down for a few seconds, collecting her thoughts, uncertain of how much she should share. "Well, here goes," she began, and unfolded her life story – her past with Mark, her friendship with Diego and Linda, her career, her worries and fears, the baby she never had, and her newfound passion for tango. Alexis didn't take his eyes off her. He didn't move when the waiter delivered the plates one after the other, and Sarah didn't feel the need to stop.

Sarah's voice softened as she concluded her story. She let out a slow sigh, her eyes briefly wandering to a distant memory. "And that brings me here," she finished, her voice trailing off as she took a deep breath, allowing the weight of her own story to settle in the air between them.

There was a moment of silence, filled with the ambient sounds of the bustling city. Alexis's eyes were full of understanding as he finally spoke. "I'm sorry you've been through so much. It must have been hard."

"Life finds a way, especially after making tough decisions," Sarah replied.

Alexis nodded and stayed silent. They both turned their attention to the array of dishes in front of them.

"How do I eat this?" Sarah asked, eyeing the baked feta cheese.

Alexis cut a small piece, dipping it into the honey and sesame seeds. "Close your eyes and just taste," he encouraged.

Sarah leaned forward, her senses heightened. The aroma of the sesame seeds wafted through the air, and she felt her mouth getting wet. The outer layer of baked feta provided a satisfying crunch when she took the first bite, while the gooey interior melted. The honey's sweetness intertwined with the rich, tangy essence of the cheese.

Sarah felt the subtle nuttiness of the sesame seeds and let out a contented sigh.

"Should we get another one?" Alex joked.

"I think I've talked enough for now," Sarah said with a laugh and grabbed her spoon. "Your turn. How did you get into tango?"

"About fifteen years ago, three friends and I were trying out different hobbies. Basketball, martial arts, juggling, ballroom dancing, you name it. One day, one of them suggested a tango class. After just one class, I was completely hooked. We dropped all the other activities and just focused on tango. I ended up attending four to five classes a week for a year. A few years later, a friend invited me to start teaching beginners at his tango school."

Sarah paused her eating. "You didn't need a certification for that?"

"Not in tango," Alexis said. "Once dancers become proficient enough, they often start by giving private lessons. Then maybe they form small groups or teach in Latin dance schools. Their understanding of Argentine tango is typically deeper than that of most Latin dance instructors."

"Why is that?" Sarah asked.

"The Argentine tango taught in most Latin dance schools just skims the surface. Often, people who start there have to go back to the basics at a dedicated Argentine tango school to really progress."

"Do you enjoy teaching?" Sarah asked, leaning in with interest.

"Teaching was the fastest way to improve my own tango. You really understand something only when you can teach it effectively to others. And it's incredibly rewarding to see people who never thought they could dance enjoy a milonga."

"So where do you teach now?"

"I don't have a fixed base. I travel the world, teaching classes," Alexis replied.

Sarah set down her fork and knife, a dreamy look in her eyes. "So, you travel, teach, and then dance some more at night?"

"That's about right. But it's not always easy," Alexis admitted.

"I'd love to have a life like that," Sarah confessed.

"What's stopping you?" Alexis asked, looking directly into her eyes with a penetrating gaze.

123

Sarah gazed back silently for a moment, contemplating. "I hardly understand my own tango. I've only been at it for a few months."

Alexis's eyebrows shot up, and he leaned back slightly, a look of disbelief crossing his face. "Just a few months? You are joking, right?"

"No," Sarah replied, a slight shrug in her shoulders.

A spark lit up in Alexis's eyes, and his smile widened. "Would you really want a life like this?"

"Who wouldn't?" Sarah mused.

"What's stopping you?" he repeated.

The waiter returned, skillfully making room for more dishes on their table.

"We should probably focus on eating for now," Sarah said with a smile.

They enjoyed their meal in comfortable silence, the clinking of their utensils blending with the surrounding chatter in a language Sarah didn't understand. Occasionally, pedestrians paused to observe their table, considering the restaurant for their own meal. A toddler in a football shirt adorned with a German flag eyed their French fries. Alexis winked at him, and the boy boldly grabbed a fry, his face lighting up with joy. His mother hurried over to apologize and pull him away.

"No problem at all. We could use some help finishing these," Alexis joked, offering the boy a piece of pita as well.

Sarah watched the boy skip away, his hands full of unexpected treasures.

"Their honesty is something I really miss in this world," Alexis said. "They wear their emotions on their face and say what they think."

"Do you ever think about having children?" Sarah asked.

The joy in Alexis's eyes dimmed, replaced by a somber shadow. Sarah wondered if asking this question on their first date was too much for him.

"Would you like to go somewhere with me after dinner?" he asked after a brief pause.

"What do you have in mind?" Sarah asked.

"Somewhere with a view."

124

They finished their dinner, and Alexis asked for the check. When it arrived, he reached for his credit card.

Sarah stopped him. "We'll split it," she said.

"Okay," Alexis smiled, "although you did eat more than me."

"In the past, I would eat before going on a date to avoid looking greedy at the restaurant. I guess I'm out of practice," she smiled back.

"Food is important," Alexis said. "There's still a pepper left. It'd be a shame to waste it." He winked at her.

Sarah quickly skewered the pepper with her fork. "These peppers are amazing, just a bit too salty, though."

Alexis unlocked his car, a white Golf. It was awkwardly parked half on the pavement of a narrow street, as all cars were, to allow space for others to pass. He put on some gentle electronic tango music and drove in silence for about ten minutes.

Sarah observed the red traffic lights sequentially turning green, creating a wave-like motion forward. Most stores were closed, secured behind security shutters. She noticed a few homeless individuals sleeping on metallic ventilation grilles on the pavement.

"The warm air from the metro below comes out from there," Alexis said. "It keeps them warm at night when the temperature drops."

Eventually, he turned right onto a street and ascended a hill. After navigating a few curves, Sarah saw the road end in an expansive open space. Cars were parked on the right, with many couples either seated inside or standing outside. Alexis found a free spot and drove towards it. As they neared, Sarah's mouth dropped open at the breathtaking panoramic view of Athens sprawling below.

"Welcome to Lycabettus," Alexis said, turning to her with a soft smile as he switched off the engine. He stepped out and perched on the hood, inviting Sarah to join him.

Sarah gazed at his broad back, which formed a dark triangular silhouette against the backdrop of the city's twinkling lights. She got out and sat next to him. For a few minutes, they silently watched the city, listening to the blend of distant city sounds and murmurs.

How did I get here? she wondered. *In Greece, jobless, without Mark, gazing at a city I've only read about in history classes, sitting next to a tango dancer I met just one night ago.* "I feel so calm here," she finally said. "It's as if I've been here before, maybe in another life."

"It's a beautiful city," Alexis remarked. "Pure chaos when you're in the middle of it, but from a distance, it's just magnificent."

"No," Sarah said, "it's not just the city. I've felt this calmness in your car, in the restaurant, in the milonga. I feel so peaceful here... next to *you*." She continued gazing at the distant lights.

"Me too," Alexis replied, his hand moving to hold hers, their fingers intertwining.

A minute later, a cold breeze made Sarah shiver.

"I've got a mini blanket in the car," Alexis offered.

"I have a better idea," Sarah said and gently pulled him off the hood. She unzipped his leather jacket and wrapped her arms around his back, feeling the soft lining. She nestled her head under his jaw, his arms encircling her. Together, they looked out over the city, gently swaying.

"You didn't answer my question before," she said.

Alexis remained silent.

"I have another question, then," she said. "The women in the class were surprised you asked someone on a date. Why?"

"It's for the same reason I didn't answer your previous question," Alexis replied.

"Are you a man who keeps his word?" Sarah asked, a faint smile playing on her lips.

"I am."

"Earlier, I said you owe me one, and you agreed to 'anything I want', right?"

"I guess I did."

"Then I want to know."

Alexis remained silent for a few seconds. "Her name was Artemis. I met her at a milonga. There was a fire in her eyes when she danced, a spark. For a few years, she was my dancing partner. We were best friends, taught together, traveled. A couple of years later, we became a couple in life too. It's not easy to have a child when you're a traveling tango teacher, but we both wanted it. So, we went for it." Alexis's hands trembled slightly as he paused, taking a deep, steadying breath.

"Those first months when her belly was growing were the happiest of my life. When we were dancing, I was dancing with her, but not only with her. I knew I was dancing with the life inside her. Everything I loved was in my arms."

Sarah felt uneasy in his embrace, unsure if she should continue hugging him or pull away. He was talking about what sounded like the love of his life.

"After a routine appointment, the doctor told us there was some incompatibility between her and the embryo. We tried a few things, but nothing worked. They said the chances of its survival were almost zero. They couldn't say exactly when. Days, weeks, a couple of months. The last time I danced with them was almost five years ago. After the milonga, she felt something was wrong. We went to the doctor. She was right."

Sarah's heart clenched as Alexis's story unfolded. She imagined the depth of his loss, her own recent heartaches paling in comparison. Words failed her. What could she say in the face of such a loss? She wanted to reach out, to offer some comfort, yet she hesitated.

"After... After that, we... We just couldn't... We grew apart. Seeing each other just reminded us of..." His voice trailed off, and his chest moved up and down rapidly with every breath.

Sarah's eyes widened. "I... I had no idea," she stammered, her voice laced with regret. "I wouldn't have brought it up if I'd known..."

She synchronized her breath with his. Gradually, she slowed hers down, feeling his breathing calming in tandem. She pulled her head back to look at him. His eyes were wet, gazing at the sky.

"You see that star there? The bright one," he pointed upward. "It's called Betelgeuse. It was the first star I saw after leaving the hospital that night. In my heart, my baby is there."

Sarah gazed at the star for a while. The evening chill began to seep into the air, contrasting with the earlier warmth. She shivered slightly, her breath visible in the cool night air as they sat together, overlooking the city.

"Let's go inside," Alexis suggested, "it's getting cold."

Settling into the car's passenger seat, Sarah inhaled the faint scent of leather mixed with a hint of Alexis's cologne.

"Are you thirsty?" Alexis asked a few minutes later.

"Yes, that last pepper was too salty."

"Don't worry, I got you covered," Alexis said, retrieving a plastic bag from the back seat. "Please hold this," he said, placing a water bottle on Sarah's lap. "And this." He put a tiny plastic cup in her right hand. "And this," he concluded, placing a bag of peanuts in her left hand.

Sarah smiled. "Airplane food!"

Moments later, they looked at each other, and Sarah's expression turned serious again.

"I am sorry I insisted. And thank you for keeping your word."

"I *wanted* to tell you," Alexis said, turning his head toward the city. "Also, Vaggelis already told me you were late too."

Chapter 22

"And?" Linda asked, holding her breakfast bowl in front of her.

"He plans to travel to Portugal and Spain to teach for a while. Then France. His whole life is tango now."

"I don't care about that. Did you...?"

"No."

"Not even a kiss?"

Sarah lifted her shoulders.

"Is he playing hard to get?"

"He was the one who asked me out, remember?"

"Something must be holding him back."

"He asked if we want to join him at an open-air milonga tonight," Sarah said.

"It's the only milonga there is. Text him we are going."

Sarah unlocked her mobile and her smile disappeared. "I have a message from Mark."

"What is he saying?"

"Where are you? I need to talk to you," Sarah read.

Linda stood up and took her bowl to the sink without saying a word.

"I can't do this yet," Sarah said.

"Tell him you are going to a milonga tonight, you can talk tomorrow."

"Don't you think it's too much to mention tango as the reason we can't talk?"

Linda looked at her and raised her eyebrows. "Tango *is* the reason you can't talk."

Sarah nodded. "OK." She typed quickly and sent the message. Then, she opened a new chat. "It feels so weird to text one and then the other."

Linda smiled. "Once I had to put one call on hold to talk to the other. You are single now, get used to it."

"I am not like this," Sarah said. "I don't want to hurt him more than I already did."

"You are just going to a milonga, Sarah. Send the damn message and let's go see the Acropolis."

An hour later, they arrived at the Acropolis, the early morning sun casting a warm glow on its ancient stones. After a quick ticket purchase, they began their ascent.

Sarah stopped in front of a small theater, its ancient stones whispering histories of performances past.

Linda read the sign. "It's the theater of Dionysus, the god of wine-making and ecstasy. Now this one sounds like a fun guy."

"Can you imagine the people here, dancing, two thousand years ago?" Sarah mused, doing a little dance. "Right where we are standing now."

As Sarah ascended the ancient path, the sun cast a warm glow on the weathered stones of a majestic amphitheater. She admired the stark contrast of the honey-colored marble against the verdant surroundings and took a moment to breathe.

"Now that's a place to organize a milonga," Linda said. "The sound of violins here would be spectacular."

Sarah closed her eyes and imagined herself dancing tango in the middle. Thousands of silent spectators watching her from around. A single spotlight on her and her partner. As they walked up the final stairs towards the Acropolis, Sarah felt thankful for wearing her white sneakers and a light romper. The Parthenon was in the middle, already surrounded by tourists taking pictures. Sarah noticed on the left a lonely olive tree next to a small temple. The statues of six women held up the building, wearing simple tunics pinned on each shoulder. She gestured for Linda to approach the building.

"They are beautiful," Sarah said, admiring intricately braided and luxuriant plaits cascading down their backs.

"It says here they are replicas. The real ones are in the Acropolis Museum. Five of them. The sixth is in the British Museum in London. Five sisters, waiting for the sixth one to come back," Linda said.

"At least she got to travel," Sarah said.

After their journey around the Acropolis, they descended towards the city's heart, finding themselves drawn into the lively embrace of

130

a bustling open-air market. A collection of gold and silver earrings caught Sarah's attention.

"Can I help you?" an old woman dressed in black asked.

Sarah pointed at a pair of gold olive tree leaves.

"The leaves, good choice," the lady said. "Did you already see the olive tree in the Acropolis?"

Sarah nodded.

"The first tree in the Acropolis was planted by the goddess Athena herself. Two thousand five hundred years ago, the Persians burned down the Acropolis. But the next day, the olive tree sprouted a new branch." She poured some alcohol on a napkin and disinfected the earrings. "Many invaders came after them, and the tree was burned many times. But a sprig was always saved to be replanted later. The tree in the Acropolis is a direct descendant of the one the goddess planted. Try them on."

Sarah placed the earrings on and looked at a tiny mirror. The golden leaf hung elegantly next to her neck.

"I'll take two pairs, please," Sarah said and glanced at the lady's other stall. Miniature copper statues, meticulously crafted, captured the essence of ancient gods and mythical creatures. Among the many items, Sarah noticed a statue that looked like the one on Alexis' tattoo. "Who is this one?"

The sun reflected on its surface as the lady lifted it above their heads. "That's Orion, the hunter, son of Poseidon. He fell in love with goddess Artemis, but she was not interested. Poor Orion, he didn't back down. She called a scorpion to bite him. He died, and up next to the stars he went too. In the night sky, Orion and Scorpius are positioned on opposite sides. When one rises, the other sets, chasing each other forever. That would be eighteen euros."

Sarah paid and placed Orion and the earrings in her bag. "Do you know any good places to eat?" she asked the old lady, who pointed to a restaurant to her right.

"Good and cheap," she said.

The small restaurant, nestled among the winding streets, welcomed them with the inviting scents of oregano and lemon. They chose a table outside, basking in the Mediterranean ambiance. Over plates of moussaka and dolmades, they chatted about the day's adventures and the evening ahead. The relaxed pace of the meal under the soothing Greek sun, combined with the anticipation of the milonga, made them sleepy.

"How about a nap before tonight's milonga?" Linda proposed as they finished their meal.

Sarah, feeling the warmth of the sun and the comfort of a full stomach, nodded in agreement.

Post-lunch, they retreated to their apartment. As they lay down, the events of the morning—the ancient stones of the Acropolis, the vibrant market, the intriguing tales of Greek history—seemed to blend into a dreamy haze.

Chapter 23

A few restful hours later, stepping out into the cooling evening, they found the city transformed. The night's energy was palpable as they made their way to the open-air milonga. The rhythmic pulse of tango music greeted them. Couples moved gracefully on the makeshift dance floor. The square, alive with the spirit of the milonga, was a tapestry of people lounging on picnic blankets, their laughter and conversations mingling with the music. Amidst the crowd, Sarah's eyes quickly found Alexis, seated casually under a tree, accompanied by an unfamiliar face.

"Beautiful earrings," he whispered in Sarah's ear as they enjoyed a prolonged hug.

Linda cleared her throat to interrupt them. "Will you introduce us to your friend?"

Alexis hesitantly left Sarah's embrace. "Please meet my friend Michalis." Michalis stood up, and both Sarah and Linda smiled and glanced at each other. He was a head taller than Alexis. "Have you seen the guys in front of Syntagma Square with the traditional Greek uniforms? He is one of them."

"We didn't have the chance yet," Linda said. "But I would love to know about those uniforms. Michalis, do you dance?"

Sarah shook her head, watching them walk toward the dance floor.

"She came to see the monuments," Sarah whispered.

Alexis burst into laughter.

"This is a wonderful place," Sarah said. "Would you like to dance?"

"It's better not. Do you see those two guys standing there? Pickpockets. If our stuff stays unattended, they will grab it and run."

Sarah looked at them. They seemed to be casually chatting, but she noticed their eyes moving fast, left and right, observing each movement in the park.

"Does that happen often?"

"Not so much anymore. We have a few of our guys standing on the corners keeping an eye on them," he pointed to a couple of them. "Usually, when we start running after them, they just throw the stolen items and run away."

They sat with their backs against the tree and watched the dancers. Sarah allowed her elbow to touch his, and he responded by letting the side of his right leg touch hers. A few minutes later, Linda and Michalis came back laughing. Linda kept her arm around him as they chatted during the cortina. When the next tanda started, Alexis gave a desperate look at Sarah as Linda pulled him by the hand to the floor. Sarah smiled and gave him the thumbs up.

"I'll stay with the stuff," she said to Michalis. "Go dance."

She watched Linda's and Alexis's lips moving as she danced. They seemed to be having a conversation. When the first song ended, they both looked at her and then went back into their conversation.

Sarah turned her head away, watching the pedestrians walking by. Every now and then, a few of them stopped and watched the dancers for a few moments. She saw the eyes of a woman mesmerized by what she was seeing. Her boyfriend, on the other hand, was trying to pull her away.

Then she noticed a man approaching. *It can't be*, she thought. He saw her. Step by step he approached, and Sarah's heart started beating like crazy. She stood up, feeling her knees trembling.

"What are you doing here?" she asked.

"I said I wanted to talk with you tonight. You told me you were planning to be at the milonga. I came here."

Sarah looked at Mark. "I don't... But... How?"

"I arrived this morning. I found this place on a local website. Can we talk somewhere, alone?"

Sarah heard the music stopping and, terrified, saw Alexis approaching. "Yes, let's go," Sarah said, taking a step away from the tree.

"That way," Mark said, pointing toward a bridge in the opposite direction.

Sarah turned back and looked down as she walked through the dance floor. She saw Alexis' legs as she passed next to him but didn't find the courage to look up. They walked up a few stairs leading to a small bridge above a metro line, and Sarah was painfully aware that everybody could see them. To her relief, they crossed the bridge and turned to the left, getting out of sight. "I can't believe you are here," she said.

They walked together for a few minutes as he explained the last-minute changes, buying the tickets, informing his boss he had to travel, and the traffic in Athens. Sarah caught herself not paying attention, her heart still beating hard, unsure what to make of all this. They walked past a few restaurants and started going uphill. The Acropolis appeared on their left, illuminated from all sides, offering a strong contrast to the dark sky around them, accompanied by a full moon.

Sarah stopped next to an olive tree. "Why are you here, Mark?" she asked.

Mark took a deep breath. "Those days were some of the worst days of my life, Sarah. I did some thinking. You were right about so many things. I am sorry. I put my career in front of everything. But that's the old me. I promise. I talked with my boss. I'll work only part-time. I want to give you the life you wanted."

Sarah felt her heart racing as she looked into his eyes, the eyes that she knew so well, that she had fallen in love with. She looked at his mouth and remembered the first time he laughed when they met, the endless hours they talked about their future and life. "What is it that you want?" she whispered, tears streaming down her cheeks.

Mark moved between her and the Acropolis and held her hands. "I want to be with you, live with you, sleep with you. I want us to forget about tango and travel. I want us to finally use the baby room for what it was designed for. Sarah, a few years ago we made some plans. It was my mistake we didn't follow up on them. I am sorry. If you are willing to give me another chance," he said and took a step back.

Sarah saw the Acropolis and the moon behind him as he kneeled.

He lifted his right hand, holding a little black box. The pedestrians around them stopped and went quiet.

Sarah looked at the ring, sparkling under the street lights.

"Sarah," he pronounced each word slowly, "will you marry me?"

Sarah looked at Mark's face and touched his cheek with her arm. Then she looked at the olive tree. She looked at the moon, and she looked at the Acropolis. She looked at the first stars appearing in the sky. She looked. And then, she looked down at his face again. "I won't stop dancing," she said.

"Is it that important for you?"

"It's part of who I am."

"I am giving you everything you wanted," Mark said and stood up.

Sarah put her hand on his cheek again. "You don't see it, do you?" She looked down. "I am sorry."

She turned and walked away. Her heart beat so hard she could feel the blood pumping through her ears. A few steps later, she started running. The wind pushed her tears back, trailing up to the back of her neck. She turned through the narrow street they had come through and kept running. She crossed the bridge.

"What happened to you?" Linda asked, taking her in her arms. "Poor thing, you are shaking."

"Where is Alexis?" Sarah asked.

"He asked me who was the guy with you. I told him. He left. But he gave me this."

Linda handed Sarah a small piece of paper. Sarah opened it. Then, she grabbed her bag and ran down the street. Seconds later, she gave the taxi driver the paper.

She looked at the lights, the pedestrians, the graffiti on the walls. Her breath blurred the window. She rolled the window down and glanced at the old buildings, dirtied by the millions of cars passing by, carrying people to important and insignificant events of their lives. The wind hit her face again, pulling her hair back. She saw couples holding hands, young people drinking and laughing, store owners closing their shops. She breathed in the air of a city that she now knew she loved. She held the air inside for as long as she could and then let it all out.

The driver stopped. With steady steps, she approached a building and ran her fingers through the intercom buttons. She found the one and pressed it.

136

Without a response, the door opened. She ran up to the third floor. Breathless, she arrived. Alexis was at the door of his apartment. She took a deep breath and stood in front of him.

"Nothing is stopping me. I am here. How do we start?"

If you have never danced tango, this page is for you. If you already dance tango, check the next page:

Sarah's tango journey is just beginning. Take a moment to visit whentheembracewhispers.com/resources to sign up for updates about the release of the second book.

But what about YOUR tango story?

I'm speaking straight from the heart here. Age, number of left feet, weight, race — none of these matter. **YOU can dance tango**. I've witnessed people who are overweight, one who was 102 years old, individuals who are blind, and even people using wheelchairs, all dancing tango. Introverts adore it because they can dance without needing to talk; extroverts love it because they can connect with people all around the world.

Argentine tango has brought me and hundreds of thousands of others moments filled with meaning, friendships, laughter. It's been a source of peace, excitement, joy, and yes, even a way to express sorrow, sadness, loneliness. It's offered us a beautiful chance to embrace and be embraced.

So, this is for you:

Visit whentheembracewhispers.com/resources

There, you'll find:

• A list of tango teachers worldwide. Reach out, take a class.

• Checklists, online tango classes, videos, guides, and other resources to assist you in your tango adventure, no matter where you live.

Take that first step. It could change your life.

P.S. If you enjoyed this novel, please write a review on Amazon, and then go to whentheembracewhispers.com/resources and let me know. I have prepared something for you. Your feedback helps more people discover and enjoy the book. Additionally, if you have any suggestions for improvement, let me know at the same link.

If you're already dancing tango, this is for you:

Sarah's tango journey is just beginning. Take a moment to visit whentheembracewhispers.com/resources to sign up for updates about the release of the second book.

While you're there...

You'll also discover an array of tango resources — checklists, videos, guides, tango stories, and more. Plus, you'll find a comprehensive *list of fantastic tango festivals, marathons, and encuentros worldwide, as well as a directory of tango teachers ready to assist you.*

...And...

If you know someone who hasn't yet experienced the joy of tango, tell them about this book or buy a copy for them. If you want, you can also simply post the link whentheembracewhispers.com on your social media.

Together, we can spread the magic of tango to even more people across the globe.

The Curious Tanguero

If you want to join me in this journey of exploring tango, and receive weekly tango tips and stories, I invite you to join my newsletter, thecurioustanguero.com

P.S. If you enjoyed this novel, please write a review on Amazon, and then go to whentheembracewhispers.com/resources and let me know. I have prepared something for you. Your feedback helps more people discover and enjoy the book. Additionally, if you have any suggestions for improvement, let me know at the same link.

Book recommendations

All books are available for **worldwide delivery** and can be purchased from **Amazon**. You can also find **links** to them at whentheembracewhispers.com/resources

Tangofulness: Exploring Connection, Awareness, and Meaning in Tango
Available in 12 languages – paperback and kindle
There are few tango dancers that haven't heard about this book. If you see in tango a way to understand better yourself and others, then this book is for you.
www.tangofulness.com

Tango Tips by the Maestros
Available in English, Spanish, Italian – paperback and kindle
This is a collection of advice from over 40 experienced tango teachers, judges of the World Tango Championship, and world champions. The maestros covered topics such as musicality, elegance, connection, balance, embrace, trust, personal style, reducing tension, creating warmth, dancing more, learning faster, and breaking through the plateau that keeps some people's tango the same.
www.tangotipsbythemaestros.com

How to dance more in milongas – for followers
Available in English, Spanish, French – paperback
If you believe that the most important criteria men have to dance with someone is age and attractiveness, don't read this book. After asking over 15,000 social tango dancers, men and women, how they choose with whom to dance in a milonga and what they do differently that makes them dance more, this book showed how those we wouldn't expect to dance much, seem to be dancing all night.
www.thecurioustanguero.com/howtodancemoreinmilongas

Letters to a tanguero

Available in German and French – paperback

A collection of advice I wish I had received when I started dancing tango. It would have saved me years of trial and error.

www.letterstoatanguero.com

Tangothoughts: My Tango Notebook

Available in English - paperback

This tango notebook will help you keep track of your progress, remember what you learned in classes or books, and accelerate your learning journey. It includes key questions designed to help you make each piece of advice or realization actionable, clearer, and memorable.

Available on Amazon

A hand upon a chest

A hand upon a chest,
Is not merely a hand on a chest.
It's not, I assure you.
If you haven't felt it,
It's more, so much more.
It's a silent whisper, 'I need you.'
There's power there,
Silent, yet flowing with an unstoppable force.
I promise you,
The bones guarding your heart
Choose to open, no longer a cage,
Allowing the hand and the heart to touch.
Because the truth is,
The hand is never just on the chest.
It's always touching the heart.

Dimitris Bronowski

About Dimitris:

Hi.
This is where people usually speak about themselves in the third person. Dimitris did this and that. Look at how cool Dimitris is. And, in case you didn't know, Dimitris also...
Well...
Dimitris has only two things to ask you.
Find your tango, and help others find theirs.
It's with light that we fight against darkness.
Bring your light.
You never know whom you might end up helping or whose life you might make a tad better.
That's what truly matters.
Also, Dimitris knows how to cook an amazing mushroom and chestnut soup.
Enough reading now.
Let's go and hug someone.

Till the next time we meet,

Always remember to hug, and let go, hug, and let go.

The first will bring you happiness, the second peace.

Dimitris

Printed in Poland
by Amazon Fulfillment
Poland Sp. z o.o., Wrocław

30951956R00090